BOOKS BY STEPHEN DOBYNS

NOVELS

Saratoga Longshot   (*1976*)
A Man of Little Evils   (*1973*)

POEMS

Concurring Beasts   (*1972*)

SARATOGA LONGSHOT

SARATOGA

LONGSHOT

STEPHEN DOBYNS

New York   *1976*   **ATHENEUM**

Library of Congress Cataloging in Publication Data
I. Title.   PZ4.D638Sar3   [PS3554.02]
813'.5'4   75–33881

FOR DON & MINNIE MAE

"You don't want to stay down here steaming like a clam. We can clear out, go up to Saratoga for the races. That's where I'm heading for. I wouldn't be here this long if it wasn't for you. You got me roped and tied, seems like."

"Saratoga? Is that a nice place?"

"July and August there's nothing like it in the whole country. Races every day, gambling, millionaires and pickpockets and sporting people and respectable family folks and politicians and famous theater actors and actresses, you'll find them all at Saratoga."

EDNA FERBER
Saratoga Trunk

MONDAY

1

CHARLIE BRADSHAW was leaving Saratoga. It was his birthday and he was going to New York City. Charlie was forty-one years old.

The Adirondack Trailways bus pulled away from the Spa City Diner, turned right onto South Broadway and headed out of town, gathering speed past the Washington, then the Lincoln Baths. Trying to get comfortable, Charlie shifted in his seat and banged his knee against the ashtray attached to the seat in front of him.

The fact of his birthday and the trip to New York were coincidental. His birthday, however, made the trip seem momentous, as if it were a present he was giving himself: something he had deserved a long time and at last decided to take.

He hoped it would be spring in New York. In Saratoga, 180 miles north, it was still winter. There had been flurries earlier that morning and it had snowed over the weekend: mostly wet snow which had melted, but Charlie could still see patches of white between the small pines of the Saratoga Tree Nursery.

It was 9:15 Monday morning, April 7. Charlie hadn't been in New York since the summer of 1960. His memory of the city was a memory of warmth.

Shifting again, Charlie bumped the man in the aisle seat. The man had refused to move when Charlie got on, forcing Charlie to climb over him. He was about forty-five and had large pink jowls that looked like the intermediate point between a silk purse and a sow's ear. A grey golfing cap was pulled down over his forehead and a grey raincoat was buttoned up to his neck. Charlie imagined he wore no shirt.

Accepting the bump as a form of introduction, the man asked, "You live in Saratoga?" And continuing before Charlie could answer: "You know, I must of come through from Warrensburg a hundred times. Always meant to stop at one of those big hotels. Put my feet up and buy a cigar. They must be torn down now. The hotels, I mean."

"There're some left," said Charlie. His mother had worked as a maid at the Grand Union Hotel until it closed in 1952.

"Should of kept them open, you know, as a kind of monument to the past. Always regretted I never stopped. Of course I saw the movie several times."

"Pardon me?" Charlie's attention had drifted to the countryside and its architecture, which, along Route 9, consisted of motels, trailer parks and a few split-levels: the seedlings of a suburbia moving up from Albany.

"*Saratoga Trunk*, there's greatness for you. I remember sitting through it time and again one Saturday afternoon as a kid until the usher came along and kicked me out. They should of kept the hotel just because of the movie. Show the world the very rooms where Clint Maroon and Clio Dulaine slept. That'd make money for them. Honest, too."

The man from Warrensburg inserted an index finger between his neck and the collar of his raincoat, pulled, then puffed out his large pink cheeks. They looked so soft that Charlie wanted to touch them.

4

The war finished the hotels. There was no racing between 1942 and 1946, and the United States Hotel was seized by the city for back taxes. The Grand Union dragged along, opening only for the races each August. Then Senator Kefauver's investigation of organized crime led to the shutdown of the gambling casinos in 1951. The Grand Union closed the following year, and Charlie's mother returned to full-time waitressing.

She had been his waitress that morning. Either he didn't know or had forgotten she was working at the Spa City Diner. He should have brought a Thermos. It always embarrassed him to be waited on by his mother.

Hazel Bradshaw was a tall, thin woman who kept her short, grey hair in tight, immaculate curls. Over the years her memory of being a maid had become distorted so that in talking to her one would think she had been a guest.

The man from Warrensburg nudged Charlie. "There's a girls' school too, right?" And again he didn't wait for an answer: "Must of been a great place to grow up. Saratoga, I mean. Think of the broads." After a short pause, he drove his elbow into Charlie's ribs. "Lucky dog!"

Charlie ignored him. He preferred to think about New York, not Saratoga Springs. He saw himself embarking upon a new part of his life and wanted to keep his mind on the future. Despite this, he found himself thinking of Gladys Cheney. Not the Gladys he had seen on Saturday when she had begged him to go to New York—an overweight, potato-like woman with no teeth. He saw her as he had seen her first in tenth grade: blond with frizzy hair like Little Orphan Annie, and large soft breasts that made it hard for her to play baseball.

It had been Mrs. Cavendish, his English teacher, who had first drawn his attention to the girl by saying, "Someday a gentleman will come along and draw the lady out of Gladys."

5

Charlie had missed the pun, but at the age of fifteen he still hoped to be a gentleman. As he thought about it, he recalled that Gladys had been toothless when she returned to Saratoga in 1960 with her ten-year-old son Sammy. Charlie had gotten married several months before. It was just as well.

He considered asking his companion if he had known a Gladys Cheney in Warrensburg in the 50's, but saw that the man had tilted back his seat and drawn his golf cap over his eyes.

The bus was three quarters full and smelled of cleaning fluid. People were dozing or talking quietly. A few were reading the *New York Times*, as if to prepare themselves. There was a general hawking and coughing. Signs over the front window told him that his "operator" was J. Stone and that the bus's number was 62606.

Across the aisle a young man in a blue cap read out loud from a Berlitz *Teach Yourself Russian*. Charlie had first thought he was throwing up. In the front seat an elderly woman chatted and giggled at the driver's neck. She wore a tall white fur hat, a red coat and thick red lipstick. Like Gladys Cheney she had no teeth, and the tips of her chin and nose bent toward each other as if about to begin an illicit romance.

Charlie looked fondly at these people. He was a kind, inquisitive man who liked children. He was happy to be going to New York. Deciding to read for a while, he took a book from his pocket. Its full title was *The Authentic Life of Billy, the Kid, the Noted Desperado of the Southwest, Whose Deeds of Daring and Blood Made His Name a Terror in New Mexico, Arizona & Northern Mexico, a Faithful and Interesting Narrative by Pat F. Garrett, Sheriff of Lincoln Co., N.M., by Whom He Was Finally Hunted Down & Captured by Killing Him.*

6

Charlie knew the book well, but instead of opening it he left it in his lap and looked out the window.

The bus was approaching the bridge over the Mohawk River, which formed the boundary between Saratoga and Albany counties. Less than ten miles to Albany now. It wasn't much of a bridge, just a rise in the highway over 150 yards of water. For Charlie those people who lived south of the river were southerners, people who lived a little differently.

Charlie hoped he would have time for sightseeing in New York. He wanted to visit Water Street and see where Sportsmen's Hall had stood over 100 years before. Kit Burns had entertained his customers with battles between grey rats and terriers, while a man called Jack the Rat would bite off the heads of mice for a dime and live rats for a quarter. The bouncer had been Gallus Mag, a huge woman who punished disorderly customers by biting off their ears. These were pickled and kept in a jar behind the bar as a warning to the rowdy. The Slaughter Housers had hung out at Sportsmen's Hall, as had the Swamp Angels, the Border Gang, the Daybreak Boys and others.

As he named these gangs to himself, Charlie looked out at the rows of tract houses which formed the northern boundary of the capitol district. In the front yard of one, he saw a small boy urging a dog to pull a red wagon by pointing a gun at it: a green water pistol.

Charlie raised his book again and shifted in his seat, still trying to get comfortable. Turning, he bumped the armrest, then winced as the butt of his own gun, a Smith & Wesson .38 Special, dug into his hip.

•

2

ALTHOUGH CHARLIE HAD BEEN in the Port
Authority Bus Terminal before, it seemed unfamiliar. His
bus had arrived at 12:35 and disgorged him onto the sloping floor of the lower concourse. He was now twisting
through the crowd trying to find his way out while avoiding
a thin man in yellow robes who wanted to talk to him.
Charlie's only comfort came from the Hoffritz cutlery store.
At least he had seen their ads.

When he emerged onto Eighth Avenue, he was pleased to
discover that it was fifteen degrees warmer than Saratoga;
and even the sky, while not quite blue, was certainly trying. Springish. Fifteen years ago, when Charlie had come
to New York for what he thought of as a last fling before
his marriage, he had stayed at the YMCA's Sloane House
on 34th Street. He saw no reason not to go there again.

Pleased with the weather and excited about being in
New York, Charlie turned into the crowd of pedestrians and
headed south. He walked slowly and was constantly jostled
by people who hurried past him the way water divides
around a rock. In his right hand he carried a small, green
plaid canvas suitcase that he had bought at the Big N on
Sunday. He swung it casually as he walked, half-crippling
strangers every few yards. Remembering that Eighth Avenue had been the border of Hell's Kitchen, he was trying

8

to recall if the Gopher Gang had had 500 or 700 members.

Charlie Bradshaw was not a noticeable man. At least four inches under six feet, he was becoming stout: cherubic, his wife said, a woman who did not like cherubs. His light brown hair had begun to recede. Not wishing to be accused of hiding it, he brushed it straight back. At the moment, it was hidden by a tan porkpie hat with a red tartan band.

His face in profile was a series of forward curves; from the front it was round and thoughtful with large blue eyes. It was a smooth face that easily turned pink from cold weather, physical exertion or simple embarrassment. It was neither youthful nor handsome. "Presentable" was the word Charlie used.

His clothes were permanent press: grey slacks, an olive green raincoat over a dark grey sport coat and white shirt. His tie had wide red, yellow and orange stripes. Both it and the hat had been chosen especially for the trip, as had the brown wing-tipped shoes which he thought of as his wedding-funeral-and-court-appearance shoes.

As he passed cheap clothing stores and pizza counters, Charlie thought he hadn't seen this many people in all the time since his last visit to New York. It was like being caught in the crowd leaving the races, except that the crowd didn't disperse but stayed with him block after block. He knew if he adapted his pace to the people around him, he would have fewer collisions, and his bag wouldn't beleaguer the knees of the passers-by. He continued to amble.

Charlie sometimes thought that his most important faculty was memory, that much of his pleasure came from recollecting the past, his own and others'. Since these memories existed simultaneously, he saw the word "past" as inexact. It was more like fishing in a carefully stocked pond.

Occasionally he would even accuse himself of doing

something only to translate it into the more durable and controllable state of memory. And he knew that might be one of the reasons he had come to New York; that beyond the problems of Gladys Cheney and her son, he had felt the need on the summit of his forty-first birthday to feed and refurbish a memory grown tired of Saratoga Springs.

Walking down Eighth Avenue, he could feel his mind drawing in sensations like a plant responding to light. He saw that the New Yorker Hotel was closed and gawked at the New Madison Square Garden. He found himself expecting to see Sam Cheney, had even felt some surprise at not seeing him at the bus station. Not that Sam knew he was coming or would meet him if he did; but since he was the cause of his trip, it seemed that Sam had increased in stature or that there were more of him. Charlie might even see 15 or 20 Sam Cheneys here on Eighth Avenue.

He had last seen Sam Cheney on a summer afternoon in 1972. Late June, he thought. Charlie had just turned onto Caroline Street from Broadway, and saw Sam emerging from the Tin and Lint: a basement bar on the corner that catered to the young dog about town.

Charlie had honked and Sam ignored him. Charlie had honked again. This time Sam walked slowly over to the car. At twenty-two he was tall and thin with long black curly hair. He had on blue denim cutoffs nearly hidden by a long white Indian shirt. His feet were bare and he stepped gingerly to avoid broken glass.

"Get in."

"I don't want to be seen with you."

"Get in!"

They had driven over to a lot by Congress Park. Charlie had learned that the police were preparing to make a series of arrests for narcotics violations, mostly marijuana. Sam was known to be a minor pusher.

Charlie had not intended to tell Sam about the impending arrests, thinking it a kind of betrayal; but when he saw Sam that day he changed his mind, deciding it was more of a betrayal to keep silent.

"I'm sure you'll be picked up with the others," Charlie had told him. "I'm not telling you what to do, but if you're smart . . ."

"Don't do me any favors."

"I'm doing it for Gladys."

Sam left town. The police made a dozen arrests. A warrant had been issued for Sam but never served.

Charlie still felt guilty about helping him. Sam was the sort of uncommunicative young man whose silence seemed a general condemnation of life. This often led Charlie to go out of his way to be friendly as if to prove that things weren't so bad. He knew quite well, however, that ever since Gladys had brought Sam to Saratoga in 1960, he had been jeopardizing his own security and well-being by getting Sam out of trouble, which in fact was why he was in New York City.

Turning up 34th Street, Charlie thought of Pat Garrett's partial justification of Billy the Kid. "The fact that he lied, swore, gambled, and broke the Sabbath in his childhood, only proved that youth and exuberant humanity were rife in the child."

The same could never be said of Sam who had as much exuberance as a turtle. Sullen was how he was usually described.

In the lobby of the YMCA was a sign saying "Welcome" in six languages. Behind the sign was an office for job referrals. It was closed. A dark purple runner extended from the main entrance to the row of five elevators. Apart from the purple, most of the colors were dark tans and browns, making the lobby dim and noncommittal. Charlie thought it had been designed by a committee sworn to stamp out frivolity.

At the registration desk, a thin man handed Charlie a membership card. When Charlie had filled it out, the man said, "Eight or nine bucks?"

"Pardon me?"

"Television or no television?"

"No television."

"That'll be nine bucks."

"I don't understand."

"You get the buck back when you return your key. Let's see some identification."

"Identification?"

"Some ID. How do I know you are who you say you are, that you're . . ." he raised Charlie's card and squinted at it, "that you're Charles F. Bradshaw from Saratoga Springs? What kind of name's that? You could be anybody."

Charlie drew out his wallet. He wanted to tell the clerk that he was a policeman, that he had been a policeman for twenty years. Instead he showed him his driver's license.

The clerk barely glanced at it. "See the cashier."

The cashier's cage was a few feet along the counter. To get to it, however, Charlie had to walk an extra fourteen feet out around a red velvet rope.

Behind the bars of the cage sat a heavy woman with a crooked silver fang hanging from a thin chain around her neck. Charlie gave her a ten. She could not have taken longer if he had given her pennies. As he waited, he looked around the lobby. There were about twenty people: young dapper blacks, old down and out whites and foreign tourists, mostly orientals. The young blacks and tourists hurried back and forth; the old whites just poked along.

12

The cashier was speaking to him. "Take these and go to the last window." She gave him two receipts.

At the last window a tall black man told him to sign one of the receipts. When Charlie handed it back to him, the man gave him a key, holding it out as if it were a morsel being given to a quick animal that could snap up his fingers as well. He didn't speak.

Charlie assumed he was done. Picking up his bag, he walked to the elevator. The number on his key was 931. He felt he had passed through a ritual into a church whose members had long since lost their faith.

The elevator arrived and an elderly man in a moth-eaten purple cardigan got out. Charlie pushed the button for the ninth floor. As the doors began to close, two orientals with cameras dove through them. They laughed about it all the way up.

The elderly whites, thought Charlie, were not actually down and out. They were one step above and had all the dignity of people who saw themselves as coping rather than drifting. Some reminded him of old drunks he had known during his early days as a patrolman: feisty, isolated men whose lives usually centered around the race tracks. Invariably they would remember his father and claim his friendship.

"That man," one had told him, "he would bet on anything, just anything." And Charlie had imagined money wagered on ants crossing sidewalks and which sparrow would land first.

"Never seen such nerve. He'd lose a fortune without batting an eye."

Charlie's pleasant mood disappeared when he opened the door of Room 931. It was about six by ten feet with dark mustard walls and a white ceiling. The cracked paint was smudged with words he couldn't read, and he imagined a depressed tourist writing "help" and "despair" on the walls in Burmese.

The one window was effectively covered by curtains with a design of small overlapping rectangles of dark red, green, yellow and brown. Charlie guessed that some enterprising chimpanzee at a Texas university had spent months on it. Apart from the curtains, the only other decoration was a color reproduction over the bed showing the Maine coast with rocks and seagulls and a man pulling a red rowboat out of the water. The narrow bed with its green spread, the tiny desk and chair—all looked like they had been pilfered from a nursery school. Charlie sat down on the chair and it swayed.

He was surprised at being in the room, at coming to New York. He had decided to come less than twenty-four hours before and that too surprised him. He was the sort of man who made careful decisions and didn't trust people who acted on impulse.

Charlie thought again of Gladys Cheney; not as he had seen her on Saturday, blowzy and crying about Sam, but as he had known her in high school. There had been a warm Saturday evening in October. He had never touched a girl's breasts before, had hardly kissed a girl except at parties where it was expected. They had lain on a blue blanket under a row of tall pines: part of the rose garden of an estate at the edge of Saratoga. She had told him that Skidmore girls came there, and spoke knowledgeably of "petting parties."

Even at fifteen Charlie was aware of doing something partly in order to recollect it later when he would tell his older and more experienced cousins. The buttons on his fly had nearly finished him. He had had an orgasm a scant three seconds after entry while Gladys was still craning her

14

neck for shooting stars.

On the back of the door of Room 931 was a sheet of instructions. Charlie read: "It is expected that the residents at all times will conduct themselves in harmony with the ideals of the Association. Gambling, profane or obscene language, disorderly, immoral or unlawful conduct or the possession or use of alcohol or illegal drugs will be sufficient cause for immediate cancellation of all privileges."

3

CHARLIE SAT in a grey metal chair next to a grey metal desk. Around him in neat rows were about twenty more grey metal desks at which men sat in their shirt sleeves, mostly white shirts. Like Charlie, they wore .38's. It was a quiet room. A secretary was typing. There was the hum of fluorescent lights. There was an occasional guffaw from two men talking by the drinking fountain.

The man who went with the desk next to Charlie was across the room in a small office. Charlie could see him through the glass door laughing and joking with an older man. Charlie felt his face grow red. He could guess what they were joking about.

The desk belonged to Sergeant Ralph Benedetto. Charlie had been introduced to him in such a way as to assume that "Sergeant" was part of his baptized name. He was a square, muscular man with curly brown hair who chewed constantly on a yellow pencil. Charlie thought he had recently quit smoking. Sergeant Benedetto was a few years younger than Charlie and his shirt was a very light blue.

Charlie sat twisting a piece of cardboard with the number 37 printed on it. The card allowed him to move freely within police headquarters. It was about four o'clock, later than he had intended. Mistakenly he had taken the Broadway local instead of the Seventh Avenue express, forcing him to walk an extra seven blocks up Chambers. Then he had felt shy about barging into police headquarters, and had moped around City Hall Park trying to summon up interest in a statue of Horace Greeley.

Sergeant Benedetto came back across the room and sat down in his grey swivel chair as if there were no one two feet away staring at him expectantly. Leaning back, he cupped his hands and pressed them against his nose and mouth. He looked down at a row of seven pencils on the left side of his desk.

"Tell me," he said through his fingers, "let's talk straight. You got some chippy here in town and you took the week off to come down and see her. But so you could ball her without complications, you told your old lady you were coming down on business. And now you've come over to see us just to lower the bullshit level. Right?"

For a moment, Charlie couldn't think. Then it occurred to him to feel angry. He had come to police headquarters hoping to be accepted as a comrade from the north, not as some clown. But apart from a certain disappointment, he didn't feel much of anything.

"You can check the hospitals and . . ."

"Sure, sure." Benedetto glanced at Charlie, then looked away. He picked up a yellow pencil, put it back down and folded his arms across his chest. "This guy, this Sam Cheney, he's been gone two weeks. Right? He's about twenty-five. He lives in the East Village. He's got a history of being involved with drugs. . . ."

"Marijuana."

"Drugs is drugs. Two weeks ago Saturday his mother calls him from Saratoga. A strange man answers and says Sam Cheney hasn't been home all night. The strange man says he's worried or it's odd or some fuckin' thing like that,

17

though I don't see what's odd about a twenty-five-year-old man being out all night unless he wears an iron lung. Anyway they hang up. For the next two weeks the mother keeps calling, but nobody answers. She can't even get the strange man anymore. Right? Okay, so she goes to you, her local cop." Benedetto stopped and recupped his hands over his mouth. He stared at Charlie over his knuckles.

"Now here comes the part I don't understand. Instead of telephoning or just forwarding a request for assistance, you hop on a bus and come down here, spend your own good money for a room at the Y of all places. Tell me, what's your relationship with these people?"

"A friend of the family." Charlie tried to smile.

"You got a big department up there? This a slack season? How many men?"

"Fifty-four." Charlie considered adding that it went up to about eighty in the summer when they hired the temporaries.

"That's not much more than we have in missing persons. Look, you know the routine. Two weeks is nothing. A guy like that, what reason do you have to think anything's wrong? You're in the juvenile division up there? A sergeant?"

"Community and Youth Relations Bureau."

"I don't care what the fuck you call it. Kids is kids. You must get paid a helluva lot to make little trips like this. Don't tell me, I don't want to know."

Benedetto picked up a color snapshot of Sam Cheney that lay on his desk. It showed a young man with long black hair standing next to a large red motorcycle. A thin face with large brown eyes and full lips, a satyrish face. Benedetto held the snapshot by the very edge as if afraid that something might rub off on him.

Watching him, Charlie found himself remembering the

18

poem that Black Bart had left for the posse after holding up the Wells Fargo Stage from Fort Ross, California.

I've labored long and hard for bread,
For honor and for riches
But on my corns too long you've tred,
You fine-haired sons-of-bitches.

Benedetto tossed the picture back on his desk. "What a punk. And all you've got is his address and the name of the place he works, a men's store on Eighth Street. Jesus, we've had this guy in here a thousand times."

"Sam?"

"No, punks like him." Benedetto picked up a yellow pencil and stuck it in the side of his mouth. "Okay, okay, we'll do the hospital routine. But look, talk straight, what'd you really come down here for? You got a chippy, right?"

4

FORTY MINUTES LATER, as Charlie walked up Fourth Avenue from Astor Place, absorbing the sunlight and looking forward to summer, he thought that his wife Marge was probably in New York at that moment, although she might have left early to avoid rush hour traffic. She and her sister Lucy ran a dress shop that catered to Skidmore girls. Marge had spent the weekend in New York investigating fall fashions and Indian blouses.

Charlie's wife liked to think of herself as a strong, nononsense woman. They had an affable, childless marriage. Lucy, his sister-in-law, had married his middle cousin Robert. Charlie sometimes thought that Marge too had wanted to marry one of his three cousins, but since they had been taken she had married him as a way of getting into the family.

Marge liked the fact that he was a policeman. She saw herself as a woman of some power and having a policeman for a husband seemed proof of it. She had urged him to be active in the Lions, Rotary, the American Legion. When he had been elected treasurer of the Protective and Benevolent Association, she had bought him an expensive chocolate cake.

Charlie felt kindly toward his wife. A shy man, he felt

grateful to Marge for taking the trouble to penetrate his shyness. He knew he occasionally confused gratitude with love, but he was basically comfortable and Marge allowed him his own life, enclosing him like a fence around forty acres. He didn't need more than that, although he might want it now and then.

Charlie suspected that Marge was part of the reason he was in New York. No more than five percent of the total motivation, but still a reason. It was unlike him to pack up and leave, and it had jolted Marge when he had talked to her on the phone the night before.

"But why go down yourself? Can't you call?"

"It's a delicate situation."

"I don't see what's so delicate about Sam Cheney. You've been wasting your time on him ever since they moved to Saratoga."

Charlie could picture her sitting on the edge of the bed in some immaculate hotel room, looking angrily into the phone as if trying to catch his eye. She was a tall, severe woman who wore outfits rather than clothes.

"I feel it's something I have to do."

"Tomorrow's your birthday."

"That doesn't matter." And he had thought she would be gone for most of his birthday even if he stayed at home.

Charlie tried to imagine telling Sergeant Benedetto that he thought it a good idea to give his wife an occasional surprise. As he crossed to 13th Street, he considered his meeting with the policeman. His lingering feeling was one of regret. He knew that part of the problem was that he neither looked nor acted like an officer of the law. Instead, he might be a vacuum cleaner salesman or a clerk for an insurance company: someone who rode buses and kept a canary, who put off buying a new pair of shoes. Although Charlie had spent years trying to achieve this effect, there was still the regret. Maybe he should have given Benedetto a karate chop or eaten a light bulb.

When he had accepted the fact that Benedetto wouldn't treat him as an equal, Charlie had begun to hold back information. He would find Sam by himself. Sam was his special task, had been his task ever since Sam had been picked up for shoplifting at the age of twelve. Sergeant Benedetto wouldn't have understood that either.

Gladys had given Charlie two other pieces of information. She had told him the name of a bar where Sam often went: The Lamplighter on First Avenue near 10th Street. And she had given him the name and address of Sam's girlfriend: Anastasia Doyle who lived on 13th Street between Fifth and Sixth avenues.

Charlie was on his way to see her now and would have been there already if he had had a better knowledge of the subway system. Fortunately the day had become increasingly spring-like, and Charlie enjoyed looking at buildings, which along here were mostly small shops and five and six story red, yellow or grey brick apartment buildings with black metal railings on their front stoops. Several smaller buildings reminded him of the building that Herman Mudgett, alias Dr. Harry Holmes, had built in Chicago in the early 1890's. It had been named Murder Castle after the police had discovered within it the bodies of more than 200 women. Charlie tried to imagine a Herman Mudgett in the buildings he passed, dissecting the body of some young victim whom he had gassed in his trick elevator after robbing her of her savings.

Mudgett had been brought up in Gilmanton, N.H., and one summer Charlie had used his vacation to go over and find out where he had lived. He had been pleased to discover there were still Mudgetts in New Hampshire.

Mudgett had once been a medical student at the University of Michigan, but had been expelled after he was caught stealing the corpse of a young woman from the lab. When the watchman asked what he was doing, Mudgett replied, "Taking my girl for a walk, you idiot."

The address that Gladys had given him turned out to be a seven-story red brick apartment building with shrubbery out in front. It looked expensive and not a bit like Mudgett's Murder Castle. Charlie pushed open the glass door.

On the wall to his left were two columns of fifteen buttons with numbers but no names. Beneath the two columns was another button next to the word "Super." The buttons were purple and protruded from a polished brass plate attached to a polished granite wall. Written above in scarlet spray paint were the words, *Eat shit* and *Slash '77*. Charlie pressed the button marked "Super."

He was standing in a small lobby between two sets of glass doors. Beyond the second set of doors was a larger lobby with an elevator, a bank of mail boxes and a green door marked "Private." The door opened and through it came a heavy-set middle-aged man followed by the oldest and biggest German shepherd Charlie had ever seen. The man held the door open and the dog lumbered through it. Then both man and dog lumbered toward Charlie, who felt he had unleashed some global threat.

Reaching the door, the man mouthed a word which Charlie took to be, "Yeah?"

"Does Anastasia Doyle live here?"

The super rolled his eyes and opened the door three inches. He had on a green work shirt and green work pants. The dog collapsed behind him and appeared to go to sleep.

"Who?"

"Anastasia Doyle?"

"Who wants to know?"

"I do."

The super again rolled his eyes and closed the door an inch. "So who are you?"

Charlie showed him a badge which identified him as a Saratoga Springs police sergeant.

The super had short grey hair that grew in patches, hair alternating with pink areas of scalp like spots on a Dalmatian. He scratched his chin.

"Fake ID? What if you stole it? I bet I could prove I'm the King of Siam."

Charlie brought out a series of cards: driver's license, Lions Club, social security, Little League Booster Club. He moved his right foot so he could quickly shove it in the crack.

"Maybe you stole the whole thing. Who's to say?"

Charlie tried to look inoffensive. "Does Anastasia Doyle live here? That seems simple enough."

"She don't like the name Anastasia. Call her Stacy, she says. You sure don't know her very well."

"I don't know her at all; I just want to talk to her."

"You and a hundred other fellas." The man opened the door. "Don't try any funny stuff or I'll put the dog on you, cop or no cop."

Charlie glanced down at the dog which lay sprawled as if it had been doped. A long pink tongue just touched the floor.

"What are you going to do," he asked, "throw it at me?"

Unexpectedly, the super laughed, a single laugh: "Hah!" He bent down and patted the dog's head. The dog didn't wake.

"This dog, she killed a guy once. I keep her just for that, must prey on her conscience. Some kid, a burglar, took too long getting through that door and Queenie was all over him. She was fast then. Throw her at you. Hah. Yeah, Stacy

Doyle lives here but she don't get back before 5:30. You can wait here in the lobby. You can't miss her. She's your height, long black hair. A looker, you know? She'll be carrying books."

The super turned and lumbered back toward the green door. Charlie noticed he wore purple velveteen slippers which matched the purple of the buttons on the brass plate. Queenie remained prostrate at Charlie's feet.

When he reached the door, the super glanced back. "Come on, Queenie, get your ass up."

The dog groaned and hauled itself to its feet. Looking dourly at Charlie, it licked its chops and shambled off.

The super was right about not missing Stacy Doyle. She was nearly beautiful: black hair that hung loose past her waist, a thin face with a long straight nose and slightly slanted green eyes. Her mouth was a little large, a little out of proportion to the rest of her face, but her teeth were perfect.

She wore a bright yellow spring jacket and a short blue denim skirt. A green Indian cloth bag hung from her shoulder and in her arms were five large books. The top one was in German: The Something Hill. Charlie had spent his two years in the army stationed in northern Germany.

Stacy Doyle reminded Charlie of many Skidmore students, the sort of woman who looks well groomed even in a paper hat. The slanted eyes reminded him of Gladys Cheney.

"I haven't seen Sam in over two weeks." She stood by the elevator and looked wary.

"Do you know where he went?"

"Why do you want to know?"

"I'm trying to find him."

"That's rather obvious, isn't it? Does he owe you money?"

A strand of black hair fell across her right eye and she tossed her head, flicking it away. Charlie guessed she combed her hair so it would fall like that, allowing her to toss her head in a way she had probably seen in a Joan Crawford movie. Under her jacket she wore a white Indian blouse and around her neck was a yellow and green striped Moroccan bead on a leather thong.

"His mother's worried," said Charlie. "She hasn't been able to reach him. I was coming down anyway and . . ."

"You're a policeman?"

"A friend of the family."

Her lips, too, were like Gladys', soft and well formed, but her manner was completely different. Stacy was impatient and businesslike, while Gladys, even at forty-one, was a large, soft child.

"I thought Sam told his mother."

"Told her what?"

"About his trip, that he was going out west."

"Where?"

"San Diego. He left two weeks ago. He was going to call her or write."

"She hasn't heard a word."

Watching her, Charlie thought she was lying. She seemed one of those tense people who force themselves to appear relaxed only when not telling the truth.

"That's just like him, he never remembers a thing. But I don't see why his mother should freak."

"Freak?"

"Send a cop all the way down just to look for him."

"She didn't send me."

Stacy tossed her head again, then glanced at her watch. It had a wide red plastic band.

"Is there anything else? I've got French at 6:30 and I'm famished."

26

"Not right now. Maybe I'll see you later or something."

"Later?"

"You know a bar called The Lamplighter?" He saw the wary expression return. It was like being looked at sideways.

"It's over on First, isn't it?"

"That's right, maybe I'll see you there later."

Charlie went through the double set of glass doors and out onto the street. The sun was still shining. He felt pleased with himself.

5

THERE WERE SMALL RIPS in the arms of the brown Naugahyde chair and cotton mushrooms of light grey padding were pushing up through the holes. Charlie picked angrily at the padding while watching a man across the living room in a similar chair, although his was green. Between them against one green cement black wall was a grey Naugahyde couch. The furniture looked as if it had grown old in the office of a local doctor. A stomach specialist, thought Charlie.

Across from the couch was a thirty-gallon fish tank with a fluorescent light. Charlie could see about fifteen fish, plus a couple of snails. At the bottom of the tank was a plastic figure in an orange diver's suit. A stream of bubbles rose up from it to the surface.

Both Charlie and his companion held Budweiser beer cans. Charlie had been squeezing his and it was dented. In a day of minor frustrations, this was the first man he wanted to hit.

"Look," said the man, whose name was Victor Plotz, "so I'm a bastard. What else is new? You know, I lost two fish today. Something's eating them. I mean another fish. I think it's the fucking angelfish. Angel. That's a laugh. Those fish are children to me. Okay, so maybe I been too

28

sharp with my tongue."

Victor Plotz was caretaker of the tenement building where Sam Cheney rented an apartment. He was in his early fifties and had a round red face with grey bushy eyebrows and grey bushy sideburns and grey bushy hair on the sides and back of his head. The skin on top was bald and pink, giving his head a soft mushroom shape.

Plotz's hair reminded Charlie of the dust balls that accumulated under his bed at home. Plotz had a large bulbous nose criss-crossed with tiny red capillaries. Charlie thought these were veins and came from drinking too much. He could also see them on Plotz's round cheeks. They looked like delicate nets meant to keep the skin in place.

"What d'you know about fish?"

"Tartar sauce."

"Fuck you."

On the floor in front of Charlie was a large grey cat whose fur so matched Plotz's grey bushy hair that it seemed that one was furred or haired with the sheddings of the other. The cat was crouched, twitching its rear end and staring at Charlie, who, although he didn't exactly dislike cats, was allergic to them to the extent that his nose ran and eyes watered whenever one got too close. Cats seemed to know this and searched him out. This cat was missing its left eye, and as it stared at Charlie, preparing to leap, its empty socket twitched gently.

"I call the cat Moshe because of the eye," Plotz had told him. "She was in a fight. I don't know who won. Who the fuck cares? Whenever some fish gives me grief, I toss it to Moshe. Moshe the Enforcer. I been telling those angelfish, 'Watch out, you fuck with me and it's Moshe the Enforcer for you. Understand?' "

It was shortly after seven o'clock. Sam's building was a yellow tenement on 6th Street at First Avenue across from a complex of new high-rises. Charlie had arrived nearly an hour before and was now trying to keep himself from shouting. His only pleasure had come from a quick visit to the cemetery of St. Mark's-in-the-Bouwerie where, in late 1876, Henry Romaine stole the corpse of the rich department store owner, Alexander T. Stewart, then successfully ransomed the body back to the family for $20,000.

This crime was particularly interesting to Charlie because it was Stewart who had modernized and rebuilt the Grand Union Hotel until it was the biggest hotel in Saratoga Springs: 824 guest rooms, two miles of corridors and more than a thousand white wicker rocking chairs for its piazzas.

"All I want," said Charlie, subtly trying to kick the cat so it wouldn't jump on him, "all I want is a quick look around. Just give me the key and I'll have it back in five minutes. There might have been trouble."

The cat sprang up over Charlie's shoe and landed in his lap. He gingerly pried its claws from his trousers and dropped it to the floor.

"Long as the rent's been paid, there's been no trouble. If my boss even knew I was talking to you, he'd put my ass in a sling."

"I'm a cop."

"He wouldn't care if you were Mighty Joe Young."

"How would he know?"

Moshe gave another leap, this time landing on Charlie's chest, fastening its claws in his dark grey sport coat. Charlie pried the claws loose and tossed the cat on the floor, first giving it a quick squeeze to show he meant business. He began brushing grey fur off his red, yellow and orange striped tie.

"I've already let you go up and bother the neighbors. Look, my hands are tied. Want another beer?"

"Sure."

30

Sam's neighbors hadn't been helpful. He had talked to two: an old man who was nearly deaf and a girl about fourteen who stood in her doorway nursing a baby that looked like a small badger. Charlie had tried to keep himself from staring at her bare breast while she told him she hadn't heard any noise from Sam's apartment for a couple of weeks.

"Here." Plotz gave him another Budweiser.

"Maybe he's dead in there."

"He'd smell."

"Maybe they wrapped him in plastic."

Charlie drew his billfold from his breast pocket and took out a twenty. He held it up.

Plotz looked disgusted. "What do you think I am?"

Charlie put back the twenty. The cat was sitting as close to his feet as it could without actually touching them. It stared at Charlie as it might stare at a little bird. The eyelid twitched over the empty socket. Charlie's eyes began to water.

"Did he have any visitors?" he asked.

"Not that I saw."

Plotz stood up and walked over to the fish tank. Although only slightly taller than Charlie, he probably outweighed him by twenty-five pounds. He wore an old grey cardigan that was baggy from keeping his hands pushed down in the pockets. He looked suspiciously into the water.

"You think this diver thing's been killing the fish? Supposed to aerate the water or something. Just got it the other day. Lifelike, don't you think? Reminded me of John Paine in *Captain China*. Now there was a movie. Remember at the end when he doesn't come up? And Gail Russell. When I heard she killed herself, I don't know, I wasn't myself for a week."

Plotz crossed his arms on his stomach and began scratch-

ing his elbows. "I can just see that little diver thingy beginning to creep along the bottom the moment I flick off
the light. Nah, Sam Cheney didn't have any visitors except
for his girlfriend and that new roommate of his."

Charlie picked a bit of cat fur from his lower lip. "I
thought he lived alone."

"He did mostly. This guy just moved in."

"Is he up there now?"

"Nope, he hasn't been around either. Don't give me that
plastic bag shit. Matter of fact, I had to look in last week
to see about a pipe. Believe me, no bodies, just dust and
roaches."

Charlie still wanted to see for himself. "Who was this
roommate?"

"Just a guy. About Sam's age. He moved in almost a
month ago, maybe less. Said he came from California."

Charlie's nose began to run. Moshe continued to sit at
his feet. "What's his name?"

Plotz walked over to a small metal desk by the door. He
leafed through some papers. "Bonenfant, Peter Bonenfant.
Comes from San Diego." He put away the papers and went
back to scratching his elbows. "Been getting some mail
too."

Charlie finished his beer and put the can on the floor.
He imagined himself grabbing the cat, plunging it into the
fish tank and holding it down on the orange plastic diver.
He tried to think about Sam Cheney. He assumed it was
Bonenfant who had talked to Gladys. But Charlie still
wanted to see Sam's apartment if only to count the tooth-
brushes.

"You won't change your mind?"

"No way. Jobs is hard enough without losing one. Want
another beer?"

Charlie got up. It occurred to him that Gail Russell had

32

been his favorite actress all through high school. "Some other time," he said.

Victor Plotz followed him to the door. "Don't think me a shit or anything. I mean, you've got your job and I've got mine. What the fuck, it's a living."

"That's okay, maybe I'll be back."

Before leaving the building, Charlie again went up to Sam's apartment on the third floor. The corridor smelled of cooked food: cauliflower or broccoli, he wasn't sure which. Sam's door was brown metal and had two shiny brass locks. Charlie tried the knob and shook it. The door wouldn't budge.

6

THE SKIN OF THE WOMAN'S ASS was the color of heavy cream. A blue rhinestone chain seemed embedded in the crack. Moving slowly back and forth, the ass swung about seven feet from Charlie's face. What Charlie minded was paying $2 for a bottle of Schlitz. There weren't even any stools.

The bar was long, about fifty feet, and above it a narrow stage ran its full length. On the wall behind the stage was a floor-to-ceiling mirror that continued around two sides of the room, transforming the two dancers into hundreds.

The dancer in front of Charlie was blond, heavy and Germanic. She reminded him of girls whose heifers won prizes at the Washington County Fair. Along with the blue rhinestone G-string, she wore matching pasties, three-inch silver platform shoes and black net stockings. She danced facing the mirror, smiling at herself and gently pinching her nipples. Now and then she would lean forward and kiss her reflection.

The second dancer off to Charlie's right was doing a subtle dance with a red velvet chaise longue. She lay on her back and moved as much as a sound sleeper might move on a rough train ride between New York and Montreal. She was young and dark haired, and her rhinestones were red and silver. Occasionally she would lift a leg and point a toe at the ceiling.

The nine other men at the bar appeared bored and hardly watched the dancers. Charlie watched but was disappointed. The only music came from the jukebox: *Rock Your Baby* by George MacRae. Charlie had come expecting to hear Cozy Cole. The Metropole Cafe had changed a lot in fifteen years. He doubted they even served coffee.

He had begun to think he had waited too long in coming to New York. He had planned to have dinner, his birthday dinner, at Jack Dempsey's Restaurant, only to find it closed. Instead, he had gone to a place next to the Metropole named, apparently, Tab Pizza Custard. Eating his two slices of pizza, Charlie had looked suspiciously at the Metropole's marquee with its sign advertising *Topless Go-Go*.

The music ended and the blond dancer turned toward the bar. She stood with her legs apart, puffing her cheeks and fanning her face with her hands. Her elbows were raised like inadequate wings.

"Don't call me fat," she half-shouted to a man near Charlie. "I'm not fat, don't call me fat." Then she grinned.

The dancer on the chaise longue spread a thin smile over the ten men at the bar as one might spread a single pat of butter over several pieces of toast. The music began again. Something called *Shame, Shame, Shame*. She slowly raised her leg.

Although not usually sentimental about birthdays and anniversaries, Charlie missed the usual congratulations. He was sorry he hadn't told Victor Plotz. At least his mother had wished him a happy birthday that morning at the Spa City Diner. She had even given him a birthday doughnut filled with a jelly mixture which he suspected was rhubarb.

Hazel Bradshaw had been cheerful, telling him it was only ten days until the start of harness racing at Saratoga Raceway, and offering to lend him her copy of *Racing Form* while he waited for the bus.

Even at sixty, Hazel still hoped to make her fortune from the tracks. Often Charlie would be sitting in some restaurant when suddenly his mother would appear beside him wanting to discuss horses. She would pull out a copy of *Racing Form*, point to a trotter that had come in last at Batavia Downs and say:

"See that horse? I got a $200 piece of it. When I'm in the money, don't think I'll forget my boy."

Unfortunately, her horses too often turned out to be afraid of robins, dandelions and other horses. Not that it stopped her. A winner was always a few days in the future, while in the present she half-starved herself in order to buy fractions of animals that could be out-distanced by toddlers on scooters. During the past few years even these fractions had diminished as inflation had tripled the annual cost of maintaining a trotter to about $3,000. If one of her horses accidentally happened to win a $5,000 purse, Hazel's share would hardly amount to $100.

At least she managed to support herself. Charlie's father, as he appeared in Hazel's stories, had left the track broke unless he won on the last race. Charlie understood this, which was why he avoided gambling. He knew that given the chance he, too, would bet on ants crossing sidewalks and sparrows preparing to land. Sometimes it frightened him how easily he could enter into the role of gambler, which, for him, was half ritual and half high school play.

Whenever he went to the flat track in August, he was always careful to enter by the same gate and made sure to tip the Salvation Army lassie fifty cents for luck. But it was between races that Charlie practiced the major part of his ritual. Armed with his program and *Racing Form* opened to the past performance page, he would watch the horses being saddled under the elms, watch the horses and jockeys enter the walking ring, then watch the parade to the track. Charlie thought of it as studying rather than watching. Often he would then run inside to see how his favorites walked, trotted, cantered or galloped to the gate. Naturally he had field glasses.

Reviewing his information, Charlie would seek a logical conclusion. It was rarely correct. His indecision about two horses might be based on their colors, while a jockey with a pleasant face could lead Charlie from one defeat to another. He was impressed by the brisk efficiency of Ron Turcotte and charmed by the angelic smile of Jorge Velasquez.

Charlie approached gambling as a romantic. He wasn't betting two dollars, he was pledging his troth, and if, in the course of his wanderings, a horse sneezed, coughed or nodded in his direction, he would back it even if it were bandaged up to its elbows and stifles.

His three older cousins, The Cousins, as his wife called them, went casually to the races half a dozen times a year, and their winnings or losses rarely exceeded $10. It was just as well that Charlie and his mother had moved in with Uncle Frank, a respectable plumber, after the death of his father.

The blond dancer still faced the bar. Actually, her dancing was a form of jogging. She had large, heavy breasts that lunged up and down in time to the music. Grinning and pinching her nipples, she called again to a man near Charlie: "See, I'm not fat."

The blond dancer reminded him slightly of Gladys, as had many women he had seen that day. In high school she had been considered fast, dating seniors and boys who had quit school. Charlie, on the other hand, had collected stamps and was secretary of the chess club. He had enjoyed the way people looked at him when it became known that he was going around with Gladys Cheney. In those days she had worn tight skirts and Charleston beads, pink frilly see-through blouses over large white bras.

Charlie thought again of Sam. If Billy the Kid was as "open-handed, generous-hearted, frank and manly" as Pat Garrett claimed then Sam's only similarity to the outlaw was in his love for his mother, for Billy loved and honored his mother "more than anything else on earth." The same could be said of Sam, and it had always struck Charlie as unhealthy.

But where Billy was gregarious, Sam was solitary. Even stealing cars had been a private act. Charlie had difficulty seeing him with a roommate. Possibly Stacy had been telling the truth. Maybe Sam really had gone to California, taking his new roommate with him. Peter Bonenfant, the good child.

Charlie finished his beer. It was after nine. He had been avoiding going to The Lamplighter. In his mind he saw it as a smoky den where customers lay stretched on benches with opium pipes.

That, however, wasn't the main reason for avoiding the place. He was afraid of being disappointed. Originally he had thought finding Sam would be easy. He had seen himself as coming into the city, poking around and there would be Sam, perhaps under a rock. It had been as simple as something in a daydream.

Charlie now realized that was foolish, and as he watched the blond dancer he told himself he had to renew his decision to find Sam or quit.

The dancer's body was like Gladys', or rather as Gladys had been in 1950. The music stopped and the dancer returned to fanning her face. She had thick, well-formed legs. It seemed to Charlie that Gladys had had legs like that; not that he had ever seen her naked but there had been a class picnic out at Lake Saratoga and everyone had gone swimming.

Uncle Frank had been a quiet man, but when he learned that Gladys was pregnant he had nearly broken Charlie's jaw.

7

NO PLACE could have been more usual than The Lamplighter, despite its various pretensions, as if its owner couldn't decide between a bar for swinging singles, the thirsty proletariat, East Village intellectuals or simply turning it into a cocktail lounge. While the owner made up his mind, the bar grew shabbier and shabbier.

It was a large, dark, square room with the bar itself, a narrow horseshoe, taking up most of the center. Along the side walls were red vinyl booths and above each booth hung a black plastic pot with red plastic geraniums. Charlie questioned the judgment of the decorator who thought people wanted to look at red plastic geraniums while they drank.

The walls were papered with the large sort of theater poster found in suburban railway stations: *Pajama Game, West Side Story*. Above the bar hung a dozen red, blue and yellow lights which rotated slowly, coloring the faces of the customers beneath. The bar itself was padded with more red vinyl. At the black on the left side of the room was a Foos Ball game, and at the back on the right was a jukebox. There were fifteen people in the bar, and not one had an opium pipe.

Charlie sat at the bottom of the U, drinking draft beer.

40

He had already talked to the bartender, a thin, bald man in a white shirt and black suspenders whom people called Luke. At first he hadn't recognized Sam's name, then, when he saw the picture: "Oh, yeah, Sam, no, haven't seen him for, jeez, can't say how long."

"How long do you think?"

"Maybe three weeks, maybe a month, maybe less. You know how it is. What're you drinking?"

It struck Charlie that Sam and Peter Bonenfant were probably off on some perfectly innocent journey, say, to visit the grave of Jesse James or Centralia, Missouri, where "Bloody Bill" Anderson massacred twenty-four unarmed Union soldiers and proclaimed in the town square, "From this time forward I ask no quarter and give none."

With some embarrassment Charlie realized he had come to New York hoping for the worst, at least to find death or disfigurement, something to justify his trip. He was not, after all, wearing his revolver just to visit places like the Metropole Cafe.

"Do you know where he might have gone?"

Luke shook his head. "Not me, I don't believe in asking questions."

There were nine other people sitting at the bar, all close enough to hear anything Charlie said. They could have been store clerks, students or factory hands. With one exception, they seemed indifferent to his presence.

Ever since he had come in, Charlie had been aware of a man watching him from the left side of the bar. Charlie thought he was about fifty. He had a large square head with grey hair brushed straight back and blue eyes that were too far apart. He wore a dark green blazer, light green shirt and a yellow tie. Theatrical, thought Charlie.

Whenever Charlie had looked at him, the man turned away, but each time he turned a little less, as if trying to

41

overcome a certain disinclination or shyness. Now when Charlie glanced at him, the man looked back and smiled. Then it was Charlie's turn to look away as it occurred to him that the man might have nothing to do with Sam Cheney, but rather thought Charlie was trying to pick him up.

It was too late. The man got up and walked toward him, bringing his drink and still smiling. He looked like an elderly but still handsome frog. Sitting down next to Charlie, he put his drink on the bar. From this distance, Charlie thought the smile was a little forced.

"So you're looking for Sam, are you?"

Charlie nodded. The man gave him a card which identified him as Lawrence A. Driscoll. In the top left-hand corner was the word "consultant."

Charlie handed the card back to him. "What do you consult about?"

"Consumer relations, free lance. I'm also looking for Sam."

When Driscoll spoke, he opened his mouth more than necessary as if he thought his words so important that they needed more space than the words of lesser men.

"How come?"

Charlie wondered if Sam was involved in shoplifting again. But whatever Driscoll did, Charlie doubted he was a store detective. He had grown aware of a strong lilac scent that came from his new acquaintance.

"He owes me twenty bucks. Why're you looking for him?"

"He owes me twenty bucks too."

"Oh." There was a pause. Driscoll looked at his drink which was a Black Russian. "You acted more like a cop."

"I am a cop. Have you seen Sam recently?"

"Not for a couple of weeks. You a New York cop?"

42

"Saratoga Springs."

Driscoll seemed relieved. "Ingrid Bergman, right? Gary Cooper?"

"Pardon me?"

"The movie, *Saratoga Trunk*. You come all the way down here just to collect twenty bucks?" Driscoll had thick, grey eyebrows which he kept raising either in emphasis or nervousness.

"His mother wants to get in touch with him. I'm a friend of the family."

"Maybe he left town."

"Maybe."

"You come down all this way just because of his mother?"

"No, I had to get a new silver whistle."

Driscoll raised his eyebrows.

Whenever Charlie talked to someone, he tried to discover the person he was expected to be. When he thought he knew, he would begin assuming that personality, thereby fulfilling his companion's expectations. Usually this meant changing small mannerisms. Driscoll, for instance, seemed to think him a kind of bumpkin; and in response Charlie began to talk in a nasal drawl, slouch on his stool and wave his hands a lot. It often happened that in thinking him so transparent, people became more transparent themselves.

"Once I get a whistle," said Charlie, "I'll have to get a whole new uniform. The chief wants us to look sharp what with the bicentennial and all. What do you mean, free-lance consumer relations?"

Driscoll gave a little jump. He had the unsettled air of someone who meant to ask a favor. He seemed to have no wish to talk to Charlie.

"Oh, you know, public relations, keeping people happy.

Macy's, Korvettes, I've had a lot of experience. I'm semi-retired now, just help out my friends."

"That so. You know anything about locks?"

"Locks? What kind?"

"Cylinder locks, I guess."

"Well, you've got a plug or cylinder with about five holes in it and five pin tumblers down in the holes to keep the cylinder from turning, and when you use the right key the pins are pushed out of the cylinder which can then rotate and move the bolt so the door can be opened. Is that what you mean?"

But Charlie was no longer paying attention. Stacy Doyle had sat down on the other side of him.

8

"I'M SORRY I was rude to you earlier. I knew there
would be a quiz in French and, well, shall we sit in a
booth?" She looked past Charlie to Driscoll who was
finishing his Black Russian and ordering another. Stacy's
black hair was pinned in a bun. It made her look older.

As he followed her toward a booth by the jukebox,
Charlie asked, "Did Sam give you an address in San
Diego? Someplace you could reach him?" He tried to keep
himself from staring at her legs. She was still wearing the
short denim skirt, Indian blouse and yellow jacket.

Stacy sat down, turned and put her feet up on the seat
of the booth so her bare knees showed above the edge of
the table. There was a red candle stuck in a wax-covered
wine bottle. After digging around in her Indian bag for
some matches, Stacy lit the candle.

"No, Sam said he'd call or write. He only meant to be
gone three weeks. I've been sort of expecting him."

"Maybe he's staying with Bonenfant's parents. I take it
Bonenfant went with him."

There was the smallest pause. "No, Peter doesn't get
along with his parents. I don't know where they're staying.
What should I call you? I can't just say Mr. Bradshaw."

Charlie had always preferred Chuck as a nickname. In

45

Saratoga, however, he had always been known as Charlie. It seemed a name for cartoon characters and clowns.

"Chuck, you can call me Chuck. Did Sam say why he was going to San Diego?"

But Stacy had taken out a small pad and pencil and was writing down numbers. The turning lights above the bar brushed red, blue and yellow over her thin face, giving her three slightly different faces and making Charlie even more aware of the original.

Stacy looked up. "Chuck Bradshaw, that makes you a seven."

"Pardon me?"

"Numerology."

"I still don't understand." Charlie found himself afraid that the differences of age, place and society were too great to be bridged.

"Every letter has its numerical equivalent. I use the Hebrew system with some help from the Greek. The letters of your name add up to forty-three. Then you add the four and three to get seven."

Charlie nodded. "How did Sam happen to know this Peter Bonenfant?"

"They met once when Sam was out west. UCLA, I think. Peter was a student there."

"What does Bonenfant look like?"

"Oh, you know, thin, long hair, jeans. Just about like anyone. You're lucky to be a seven. It's one of the best numbers." She still held her pad and seemed to be consulting it.

"What does it mean?"

Stacy put the pad on the table. "It's a number of completeness and the number of the moon. Seven controls the cycles of life. The body renews itself every seven years; each phase of the moon has seven days. There are seven

46

colors in the spectrum, seven notes in the scale, seven days in the week, seven orifices in a man's body."

"What's that have to do with me?"

"It makes you who you are. Sevens are very serious, even scholarly. They stay by themselves, think and meditate a lot. You know, unworldly. They're very dignified and self-controlled. All sevens are smart and imaginative. With many people you know their number right off, but sevens are more hidden; you always think they're something else. They're aloof and don't care about money."

When Stacy spoke, she stared directly into his face, neither blinking nor turning away. The bar had become crowded, and the noise and people surrounded them like a small room, almost adding to their privacy. Charlie couldn't decide why she was telling him about numbers.

He began to ask another question about Bonenfant, then said, "Why don't you use the whole name? I mean, my name's Charles Fletcher Bradshaw."

Turning in her seat, Stacy leaned toward Charlie until her face shone and flickered in the light from the candle.

"You use the name the person is known by or how he sees himself. Numerologists believe the name of something contains the essence of its being. Your name is a miniature image of you. So to find out what a person's like, you study his name. The whole thing goes back to Pythagoras and has to do with the cycle of vibration. I'm still learning about that. Did you know the medieval Jews believed you could cure a sick man, save his life, just by changing his name?"

"No," said Charlie, "I didn't." He watched as Stacy began to write something else on her pad. Her earrings were small golden stars and reflected the candlelight. Glancing through the people toward the bar, Charlie saw Driscoll staring at him. Driscoll raised his eyebrows.

"You also have two other numbers," said Stacy. "Do you want to know about them?"

"Why did Bonenfant come to New York?"

"I don't know. He just showed up."

"Okay, tell me about the numbers."

"Well, there's your heart number and your personality number. You get your heart number by adding up the vowels in your name. You've only got three and they come out to eight. To get your personality number, you add up the consonants. Those come out to eight, too. That's rare, usually you have different numbers."

Charlie felt ignorant. "Explain," he said.

"Your heart number shows your inner self and your personality number shows your outer self. When the number's the same for both, I don't know. Maybe it means you're sincere or something."

Stacy had taken a piece of red wax from the candle and was rolling it against the table until it became long and snake-like.

"What's an eight?" asked Charlie.

"It stands for worldly involvement and either material success or failure. Eight is twice four, and four is the number of earth and matter. Four is also the number of defeat, so eight can be a spectacular defeat. But in Christian symbolism, eight is the number of life after death, so it can be success or failure, you know, heaven or hell. Eight is the number of eternity or infinity. That's why the mathematical symbol for infinity is an eight lying on its side. Eight also means new life. A woman's body has one more orifice than a man's, and that eighth hole is the child's entrance to the world. In churches the baptismal font traditionally has eight sides, meaning that baptism is the beginning of a new life. And it used to be that Jews would only name a baby boy on its eighth day."

Charlie finished his beer. "What's any of that have to do with my heart and personality?"

"It all applies to who you are. Most eights are businessmen or politicians, even policemen. They're hard workers, but they can be unimaginative and selfish. Sometimes they get mean and push people around. Often they don't like themselves. They're sure they'll fail or that other people don't like them. They can also be rebellious. You know, spend half their lives doing something, then turn around and do something else or just screw it up. But the main thing is that they will either succeed tremendously or fail tremendously. There's no in between."

"How long have you been telling fortunes?"

Stacy looked at him seriously. "I'm not predicting anything. I'm just telling you what already exists."

Charlie nodded and looked away. "What if my name were Charlie?"

Stacy wrote down some numbers. "Charlie Bradshaw comes out to eight. Great success or failure."

"How about Charles F. Bradshaw?"

After a moment Stacy said, "That makes you a nine. They've really got class. Three times three, the number of brilliance. Both Lincoln and Kennedy were nines. Tremendous mental and spiritual achievement."

"What about Sam? What's his number?"

Stacy answered without hesitation. "Sam's a five."

"What's that?"

"It stands for sexuality. Fives make the best lovers. Sensuality too because there are five senses. It's the number of Don Juan. Fives are gamblers, always moving around, taking new chances. But mostly it's sexuality."

"What's your number?"

Stacy glanced up at him. "I'm also a five." She reached out and touched Charlie's wrist with one finger. "Sevens are good lovers, too."

Charlie tried not to jump. "What do you do when you're not talking about numbers?"

Stacy laughed and leaned back in the booth. "I'm a graduate student in modern languages at NYU."

Charlie knew he was being seduced but he didn't know why. Although not ugly, neither was he particularly dashing. And even accepting the sexuality of sevens, he didn't think eights were known for much. Great success or failure. Charlie could count his sexual conquests on one maimed hand. Most had come when he was stationed in Germany.

He didn't count his wife a sexual conquest. He was a solidly married solid citizen of Saratoga Springs. Whatever his inclinations, Charlie lacked the opportunity. Even if the chance arose, his shyness would defeat him.

But Stacy seemed indifferent to his shyness. Why should she seduce him? He guessed it had something to do with Sam and he wanted to know more about that. The question was whether to agree, but even the asking of it caused him to breathe faster. Again he found himself thinking of his birthday. Stacy sat back watching him. Being an eminently polite man, Charlie wasn't sure how to say he was willing to be seduced.

Stacy solved that problem for him. Picking up her pad, she said, "Let's go back to my apartment."

TUESDAY

9

WHEN CHARLIE WOKE at seven the next morning, he at first didn't know where he was. Fully clothed except for his shoes, he lay on a blue couch, the springs of which were so broken that the pillowed surface could be converted into a roller coaster for braver mice. Charlie's back was killing him. His mouth felt dry and he thought that wherever he was, he must have been drunk when he arrived.

Then, looking across the room, he saw a double bed with white sheets and a white bedspread. Long black hair was spread out on the pillows.

Charlie sat up and pulled off the army blanket that had covered him. Wishing to be gone before Stacy woke, he began hunting for his shoes and found them side by side next to the couch. His tan porkpie hat was on top of his shoes and his striped tie was carefully folded on top of his hat.

The room was full of sunlight. Apart from the couch and bed, the only furniture was a white wooden table with several straight chairs and a small white bureau. The walls were white and bare. Along the wall by the door were ten cardboard boxes full of books.

Charlie finished tying his shoes and stood up. He looked

at Stacy, half-covered by the white bedspread. She was naked and lay on her side with her knees drawn up. Her hair was like a black fan on the pillows. Expressionless, her thin face seemed to be waiting in transition, like her half-furnished studio apartment, between two important points.

They had only talked the night before. Talked. Charlie had done most of the talking with an animation intended to make sure there were no long pauses during which she might ask him why he was sitting on the couch. At last she had gone to sleep.

He told himself he did not want to act in a way which he would disapprove of in others. He told himself he had to be careful in New York, that he wasn't taking a vacation and couldn't allow himself to let down his guard. He had also been shy, afraid of appearing a fool with a woman young enough to be his daughter. He had been afraid that he wouldn't be able to maintain or even achieve an erection. So he had talked.

He had talked about himself and Saratoga Springs as if the town were a tree and he were one of its branches. Saratoga Springs: home of Charlie Bradshaw, parimutuel betting and the potato chip. He told her how in 1830 Dr. John Clarke was shipping out 1,200 bottles of mineral water a day for such complaints as scorbutic ulcers and depraved appetite. He talked about his father's wedding present to his mother: a balding parrot named Kentucky after the first winner of the Travers Stakes. If Stacy hadn't been naked, Charlie would have shown her the scar on the back of his left hand where Kentucky had bit out a chunk when Charlie was six.

Unsure of where he was or what to do, Charlie comforted himself by describing where he had been and what he had done. He told her how he had spent the previous year's vacation driving around central New York following the trail of the Loomis gang who had raided farms from the 1840's until nearly 1900, and had sold thousands of stolen horses to the U.S. Army during the Civil War. And he was sorry he hadn't brought the photographs of the farm house in Nine Mile Swamp where George Washington Loomis, Jr., leader of the gang, had been beaten to death by vigilantes in 1865, and his brother, Plumb, had been beaten and thrown into a bonfire.

Stacy hadn't said much. She had taken off her clothes and gotten in bed. Charlie had looked away, while realizing she wouldn't have cared if he had circled her with a camera. Then she had sat in bed watching him, presumably waiting for him to join her while he had talked faster and faster. When he had finished telling about the Loomis gang, he saw she was asleep. He had taken the army blanket from the foot of the bed and covered himself on the couch. Since entering her apartment, he hadn't mentioned Sam Cheney.

Now Charlie wanted to escape. He had no experience with young women and was afraid of appearing even more ridiculous. He walked quietly to the door.

"Are you leaving?"

Turning, he saw Stacy up on one elbow watching him. He was more aware of her bare breasts than her face.

"There's some stuff I've got to do."

"I mean, are you going back up to Saratoga?"

"Not today."

He stopped as Stacy got out of bed and walked to the white bureau. She made no attempt to cover herself. The loveliness of her body was like an eraser on Charlie's mind. She drew a pair of white panties and faded blue jeans from the bureau and put them on. Charlie looked away again. He began to feel bullied in a way he wasn't used to.

"Tell me more about Peter Bonenfant."

Stacy had been slipping a rope belt through the loops on

her jeans. She stopped and looked at Charlie in surprise. She had small firm breasts with small nipples.

"I told you, he's a friend of Sam's. They met at UCLA."

"Was he a student there?"

"I think so."

"What was he studying?" Charlie carefully kept his eyes on her face.

"I don't know, sociology or psychology. Is it important?"

"It might be. Why'd he come to New York?"

Stacy finished putting on her belt. "I don't know, maybe he just felt like it."

Charlie kept pushing. "Didn't Sam know he was coming?"

"I don't think so."

"Are you sure?"

Stacy glanced at him angrily and walked over to the kitchenette. Putting some water in a tea kettle, she lit the stove and put the kettle on the front burner.

"Do you want some coffee?"

"No, thanks." Charlie didn't move from the door. "Are you sure Sam didn't know he was coming?"

Stacy turned quickly, her black hair fell across her right shoulder partly hiding her breast.

"I don't know much about it. He seemed to just show up, you know, on the spur of the moment. At least Sam didn't say anything."

"So then Sam decided to go out west?"

"That's right. He'd been meaning to take a vacation so he decided to go back with Peter."

"And they drove?"

Stacy nodded. Opening a small refrigerator next to the sink, she took out a bottle of orange juice. "Would you like a glass?"

"No, thanks. Where did Sam get a car?"

Stacy took a glass from the cupboard above the sink and poured herself some orange juice. She kept her bare back to Charlie. "He borrowed one."

"Borrowed?"

"That's right."

"Are you sure?"

Stacy turned and some of the juice slopped over the rim of the glass. "What the hell is this? You want to twist my arm? I thought you were a human being."

She put down the juice, walked to a closet near Charlie and took a yellow sweater from a hook. As she put it on, Charlie could have reached out and touched one of her breasts. He moved back a step.

"And you say there's absolutely no way I can get in touch with Sam?"

"I've told you, I don't know where he is. It's that simple."

Charlie found himself thinking that he very rarely saw his own wife naked. Marge changed her clothes in the bathroom, and at night she always wore men's pajamas.

"Okay," said Charlie, "I'll probably see you later."

He opened the door, paused and added over his shoulder, "I'm sorry if I kept you up last night."

10

CHARLIE GOT BACK to the YMCA at 9:30. He had stopped for breakfast and at a printers on Seventh Avenue to order some business cards:

CHARLES F. BRADSHAW
SERGEANT
COMMUNITY AND YOUTH RELATIONS BUREAU
SARATOGA SPRINGS, N.Y.

The man at the counter had said he could pick them up that afternoon. Charlie thought the cards would be useful in soliciting funds for Little League Baseball.

After paying for another night, Charlie went upstairs to change his clothes and wash. The mustard yellow halls were crowded with Puerto Rican maids pushing linen carts and shouting in Spanish.

Unlocking the door of Room 931, Charlie entered, then stopped as abruptly as if he had bumped into a second door a few feet beyond the first. A large, thick man in a grey overcoat and grey fedora sat on the small chair by the desk. He was holding Charlie's book: *The Authentic Life of Billy, the Kid.*

"You reading this?"

"Sort of, I mean, I've read it before."

The man tossed the book on the desk. "What'd you do, get laid?"

"What. . . ?"

"Bet your fucking A. you did. Sam Cheney, he's going to love you."

Charlie started to reach for his revolver. The big man casually stuck out his hand, palm forward.

"Don't do it. Jesus, Benedetto said you were a stooge. He didn't know the half of it. Big fucking cop you are."

He took out his wallet and showed Charlie his identification which said he was Conrad Zack, a lieutenant with the New York Police Department.

Charlie took no pleasure in seeing him. "How'd you get in here?"

"Through the window, you prick. You really take the cake. Why're you looking for this Sam Cheney anyway? Or have you quit now that you're balling his old lady?"

Charlie began to get angry, then thought better of it. He took off his hat and raincoat, and sat down on the bed. What bothered him most was that Zack could get into his room, while he couldn't get into Sam Cheney's. He looked at Zack, still restraining himself. The New York lieutenant was about forty-five with a square head, square chin and sagging brown eyes like a hound's. The grey of his face almost matched the grey of his overcoat and fedora. He returned Charlie's stare with a mixture of boredom and disgust.

"His mother's worried about him," said Charlie at last.

"Jesus, you fuck her too? I better cross my legs."

"You got anything special to say or are you just going to sit there and insult me?"

"I'm gonna insult you awhile longer, you dumb fuck. I want you to check out of here and go back to Saratoga Springs."

59

Charlie leaned back against the wall. "Is there anyone I can report you to for breaking into my room?"

"I told you, I want you to go home."

"I'm looking for Sam Cheney."

Zack shook his head. Then, taking off his fedora, he looked inside it as if it were the place where he kept clever remarks. His grey hair was in a crew cut. Charlie guessed it had been in a crew cut ever since Zack had gone into the Marines or army or whatever he had gone into twenty-five years before.

"Look, don't think I'm a bastard. We got something all arranged down here. If you hang around, you're going to mess it up."

"What sort of thing?"

"That's none of your business. You just believe me, that's all. If you keep poking around and asking questions, you're going to screw it up for the rest of us." He had a low nasal voice, devoid of any emotion except anger and boredom.

"What about Sam?"

Zack got to his feet. He was about six inches taller than Charlie. "You think you're Pat Garrett? You think this Sam Cheney's some Billy the Kid? What kind of game are you playing?"

Charlie kept his voice calm. "I've got to call Benedetto."

"Why?" Zack stood over him like a tree about to fall. "I talked to Benedetto yesterday, I talked to him today. Believe me, Sam Cheney isn't in any hospital, though it would be better for him if he was. You go home, okay?"

"What kind of trouble is he in?" asked Charlie.

"I don't want to talk about it."

"Drugs?"

"I said I don't want to talk about it."

"What if I don't go back?"

60

Zack held out his right hand, then slowly closed his fingers, making a fist. "What do they teach you in Saratoga? How to be a fast prick? I'm being a nice guy, okay? We'll find your punk for you. If you stay down here and step on our toes, well, there's nothing to say I gotta keep being a nice guy."

Charlie tried to think of something truly insulting; something that would leave Zack crushed. Instead he said, "Sure."

Zack stared down at him. Disdain, boredom, it wasn't a pleasant expression. Then he left.

Charlie shut the door after him, kept himself from slamming it. For a moment he stood by the door. He was a thoughtful man and he disliked anger because it interfered with thought. It made him angry not to be taken seriously.

Opening his suitcase, he rummaged around for his toothbrush and shaving gear. He found it interesting that Zack had known he had been with Stacy Doyle. Either he was having her followed or The Lamplighter was under surveillance or both. Taking out a clean shirt, Charlie grabbed a towel from the shelf and walked to the door.

As with Benedetto, Charlie would have preferred to be accepted as a fellow policeman. Indeed, it was unfortunate that Zack hadn't been more friendly. Charlie told himself that if Zack had been halfway polite, he would have gone back to Saratoga Springs. After all, he didn't want to interfere with a colleague.

As it was, he didn't see why he should allow Zack to influence him. He knew he was being stubborn, but as he walked to the washroom, Charlie told himself that Zack's problems were no concern of his.

11

AT ONE O'CLOCK Charlie Bradshaw was strolling up Fifth Avenue toward the Plaza, staring into store windows and gawking as much as any tourist from Kansas. He was particularly interested in a fifty-story building on 57th Street with glass walls that widened near the bottom forming a ten-story slide. He was curious to know what would happen to someone who jumped from the top. Would he strike the street or land in the lap of a terrified secretary on the fourth floor? Although he watched for nearly ten minutes, no one jumped.

It was a bright, sunny day, and while the air was cool, not much more than forty degrees, it had the feel of air that had blown from some spring-like place. Many people on the crowded sidewalk had their coats open, and no one had that huddled look of someone enduring the chill of winter. Charlie had walked from the YMCA to the Empire State Building and had then turned up Fifth in an attempt to improve his mood which had gotten much better by the time he reached the library.

He hadn't done much washing at the Y. In the toilet stalls were such messages as: *Sex in Room 943, Come to the showers for a big one, Sex in the showers anytime,* and *Bobo, be in the showers at one.*

Charlie felt some concern for the present occupant of Room 943. None of the messages were dated. Perhaps Room 943 now contained an asthmatic old man with a weak heart. Did he complain about people tapping on his door at 3 a.m.? Did he wonder about the sly looks of his neighbors?

Charlie had gone so far as to glance into the shower room. The walls and floor were covered with small rectangular pieces of light brown tile. No orgies had been in progress. The only occupant had been a large middle-aged man turning slowly under the water like a kind of pink walrus. Becoming aware of Charlie, the man had looked at him with scorn, actually wrinkling up his nose. Charlie had hastily closed the door and decided not to shower that day.

Pausing by the Pulitzer Fountain, Charlie glanced around for an empty bench but all seemed occupied. He was enjoying the crowds of people who on a day like this seemed friendly and less withdrawn. He watched an attractive young woman get into a light grey Rolls Royce in front of the Plaza Hotel, and he thought she might be a celebrity. She was bound to be someone. He considered telling his friends in Saratoga that he had seen—who had he seen? The women who had once excited him in films were no longer young. Princess Grace? Jane Russell? Charlie continued up Fifth Avenue toward the statue of General Sherman.

When he had left the Y that morning, he had found a message to call Stacy. Surprisingly, she had apologized for being rude.

"I'm never friendly in the morning," she had said. "Maybe we can get together later unless you're going back. Please don't think I was bored last night."

Despite his better judgment, Charlie had been flattered. "I'll be over at The Lamplighter this evening."

"What time? I'll meet you."

"Around nine." Charlie paused. "You know, when I got back to the Y this morning, I found a cop waiting for me."

"Oh?"

"Yeah, he was waiting in my room. Must have had someone open it up for him. Sort of irritated me." He waited to see what she would say. For a moment she didn't say anything. The room with the phones was a long narrow room off the main lobby. It was empty except for Charlie.

"I should think it would. Who was it?"

"A lieutenant by the name of Conrad Zack."

"He's a narc." That was said quickly.

"How do you know?"

"It's common knowledge. I mean, he's a lieutenant, isn't he? What did he want?"

Charlie had ignored this. "Has Sam been in any trouble with drugs in New York?"

"No, well, one time he was picked up at a place where some guys were sniffing coke. The police said he was loitering in the presence of a controlled drug or something like that. They let him go after a while. What did Zack want?"

"Just to say hello. Did you know Sam was almost arrested in Saratoga for selling grass?"

"I didn't know he was selling it."

"Well, he was. A warrant was issued but Sam left town before it could be served."

"I knew you had helped him."

Charlie was surprised. "Sam told you about me?" His first thought was that he had told Stacy to call him Chuck, while Sam would have referred to him as Charlie.

"Look, I've got to run. I'll try and meet you at The Lamplighter. Okay?" She had hung up without waiting for an answer.

Although Zack was a lieutenant, Charlie knew there were between 500 and 600 men in the narcotics division of the New York Police Department. He told himself that Stacy had probably seen the policeman's name in the newspaper, but he didn't really believe it.

Charlie stood near the statue of General Sherman and watched several horse-drawn carriages waiting for customers on Central Park South. Trying to forget Zack, he considered what it would be like to ride down Fifth Avenue in a carriage, leaning back and looking up at skyscrapers and blue sky. As he thought about it, he imagined himself riding in a carriage while next to it drove a police car with Zack staring from the back seat. It would do nothing to change Zack's opinion that Charlie was a punk cop, a goof.

Actually, thought Charlie, wandering into the park, I've had all sorts of training.

Over the years Charlie's chief had enrolled him in a variety of courses, ranging from new weapons to the feasibility of mounting television cameras on street corners. Since these courses were paid for by the government, Chief Peterson had thought it foolish not to take advantage of them and somehow it had been Charlie who was always sent.

Most memorable had been several weeks at the Civil Defense Agency school in Battle Creek. He had learned how to control food riots and had qualified as a fallout shelter manager. One day in class a police detective from Saginaw had nudged him and said, "You know, a shelter manager, he's got the pick of the broads."

Sometimes, late at night, Charlie would think of this policeman, waiting for the Bomb in Saginaw so he could at last attain sexual fulfillment.

Charlie asked himself how Zack would respond to the

news that he was a qualified shelter manager. Perhaps he could tell him when Zack cruised by his open carriage. It would be even better if Stacy were with him.

He continued to think of her with regret. He was sure, however, that if the moment were repeated he would still refuse to get into her bed. It remained surprising that he had even gone back to her apartment. Partly it was because of his birthday, and partly because she reminded him of Gladys. But if Stacy were Gladys, that would put Zack into the role of his uncle who was the gentlest of men, always excepting the day when he heard Gladys was pregnant.

Uncle Frank had accused Charlie of being just like his father, a cheap Don Juan who never cared about the consequences. That had been more painful than the blow for which Uncle Frank had later apologized.

Each day in school, Gladys had teased Charlie about getting her pregnant, had passed him notes accusing him of being the father of a child she was already calling Little Leroy. Charlie had been humiliated.

At the time he had had no idea that Gladys was also teasing four other boys, any one of whom could have been the father of Little Leroy. Of the five, one had left town, two had coughed up money, one had proposed and one had kept very quiet. Charlie had been the last. Uncle Frank had been certain it would end in court, although he was more afraid of scandal than legal retribution.

Then, unaccountably, Gladys' mother had taken her up to Warrensburg. When Gladys had returned, Sam had been ten years old. At least she hadn't named the child Leroy.

By now Charlie had reached the zoo. Even the animals seemed invigorated by the warmer weather. Monkeys cavorted and tropical birds made noises like nails being drawn from wood. But it was the zebras that attracted Charlie the most.

As he stood before their pen, he realized that without his knowing it the zebra had always been his favorite animal. They were so tidy, not clean but tidy in their stripes. So contained and suitcase-like. He remembered reading that they couldn't be trained for riding, and he felt it must be because no one had ever properly tried or had had enough sympathy. Charlie asked himself if, given the chance, he would rather domesticate the zebra or find Sam Cheney. The question depressed him and he moved away from the pen. He would find Sam Cheney.

12

AT FIVE O'CLOCK Charlie sat on a stool at The Lamplighter drinking his first beer of the day. He had no definite plans but he knew his presence was an irritant and he hoped something might come of that. If nothing else, it would irritate Conrad Zack. The thought gave him pleasure and he didn't bother carrying it through to its possible consequences.

Earlier, after picking up his business cards, he had gone down to the men's store on Eighth Street where Sam worked. It was the sort of place that calls its merchandise "trend-setters." One such trend-setter in the window was a three-piece, double-breasted suit of pink velveteen. With it were a pair of pink and black patent leather shoes with three-inch soles. Charlie had thought of buying the outfit and wearing it in his quest for Sam Cheney. He might even wear it back to Saratoga. Then he had dismissed the idea, somewhat unnerved by the new turnings of his mind. He was certain that the Protective and Benevolent Association would never allow its treasurer to be seen in a pink velveteen suit.

Talking to the manager, Charlie had learned that Sam hadn't been seen since Friday, March 21st. He hadn't even picked up his paycheck. It was unlike Sam to leave money lying around.

As he left the store, Charlie had been stopped by one of the clerks: a thin, emaciated young man with dyed blond hair. Charlie had felt concern for his pallor until he realized it had come from a bottle. Perched on the tip of his nose were a pair of glasses with octagonal wire rims. At first Charlie had thought they were very clean, then he realized they had no lenses.

"I don't know if you know this," the clerk had said, "but Sam was trying to raise a lot of money before he . . . left."

"How much money?"

"Oh, I don't know, maybe thousands. I mean, that's why it's funny about his paycheck. You know what they say . . ."

"A fool and his money are soon parted?"

The clerk tugged at his yellow bow tie. "I was thinking of 'every little bit counts.' "

Later, sitting in The Lamplighter, Charlie was trying to arrange his pieces of knowledge. 1—Sam's disappearance. 2—Sam's need of money. 3—Sam's involvement with drugs. 4—Conrad Zack. It seemed that either Sam was going to buy drugs or he owed money to some drug-related person. In the past, Sam's involvement had been with marijuana. Charlie would have suspected that he was again mixed up with marijuana if it weren't for Zack. He didn't think a police lieutenant would directly involve himself for a few kilos of grass.

As he considered this, Charlie wondered about Peter Bonenfant. He couldn't decide about the level of his involvement. Nor could he decide about Stacy. Although he might feel she was innocent, Charlie doubted his objectivity. Also, if Sam's disappearance had some perfectly natural explanation, why hadn't he contacted the clothing store about his check? It could easily have been forwarded to California.

69

Charlie went over these questions with growing irritation. It seemed that just as he was about to reach some new plateau of speculation, he would have a mental picture of Stacy Doyle lying naked on her white bed. Charlie disliked these intrusions: such erotic fragments made him mistrust his judgment. But even as he grew angrier with himself, he would see Stacy so clearly that it seemed he could touch her.

Charlie was fearful that he might be growing infatuated with a twenty-three-year-old woman. He thought it undignified. It wasn't that he believed being forty-one limited him to certain prescribed courses of action. Rather he wanted to remain the master of his actions, whatever they were.

A cautious man, he distrusted people who were not in control of themselves: people driven by love, anger, drunkenness or a desire to bet all their money on tenth-rate horses. He told himself that he didn't want his own life disrupted. But even as he thought that, he knew it wasn't entirely true. He knew that by coming to New York he had chosen a kind of disruption. He had chosen to leave the orderly path of his life in Saratoga.

Although Charlie enjoyed his life, it sometimes seemed as if he were leading a life that had been carefully laid out for him. His uncle had been careful to steer him away from the direction taken by his father, while his cousins, The Cousins, had helped him find the job with the police department. There had only been a few occasions when Charlie felt he had left the preordained path. Once had been with Gladys, another was this trip to New York.

Charlie called Luke over and ordered another beer. There were eight other customers in the bar, and most of the noise came from four men playing Foos Ball, slamming the metal rods and shouting whenever the ball shot past the miniature goalie. As Charlie received his beer, Lawrence A. Driscoll climbed onto the stool to his left.

"I thought you might be gone."

"No, not yet."

"Don't you get bored doing this kind of thing?"

As on the previous evening, there was condescension in Driscoll's voice; and although Charlie believed it might come from Driscoll's own insecurity, he was tired of assuming the role of bumpkin. Driscoll still wore his green blazer. Under it he had on a tight green turtleneck which made his large stomach look like half a green apple.

"Actually," said Charlie, lengthening his vowels, "actually I been sightseeing. I'll bet dollars to doughnuts you didn't know this was the northern stamping ground of The Dead Rabbits."

Driscoll's slightly indifferent expression turned to concern, then anxiety, as if he supposed Charlie was about to spit blood.

"Don't worry," said Charlie, patting his shoulder, "all The Dead Rabbits been dead for some time. They were a gang of toughs who robbed, mugged and worked for Tammany Hall in the 1850's. Their battle flag was a dead rabbit stuck up on a spear. The reason I'm interested is that for a while their leader was Old Smoke Morrissey."

"Oh?" The anxious expression subsided to mild concern.

"You see, it was Morrissey who brought big time gambling to Saratoga Springs. Morrissey's Club House made him a fortune. Later it became the Canfield Casino. Old Smoke used to tell people, 'No man can say that I ever turned a dishonest card or struck a foul blow.'

"And it was Morrissey, not Travers, who made horse racing fashionable. 'Course, once Travers saw there was money in it, he started his own racing association and pushed Morrissey out. Old Smoke's track was called Horse Haven and they keep it on as a training track."

"Is that so." Mild concern had subsided back to in-difference.

It was clear to Charlie that Driscoll had not joined him by choice. He wanted to ask, Are you a policeman? An undercover host of the city? Watching him, Charlie was reminded of a fat boy, nicknamed Salt Pork, whom he had known in grade school. Salt Pork was a lethargic child whose only enthusiasm came from opening the paper bag containing his lunch. This was a ritual that could last fifteen minutes as Salt Pork prodded, squeezed, sniffed and finally unpacked the bag as one might open a Christ-mas present from a favorite aunt. The eating was always done quickly. Weak and pimply, Salt Pork was a constant target for bullies; and Charlie felt guiltily grateful for this, thinking that if Salt Pork hadn't been the class victim, he might have been chosen himself.

Charlie put his hand on Driscoll's green sleeve. "Now you're a cultured man. I'd think you'd be interested in a rags to riches story like Old Smoke's. Did you know he was heavyweight boxing champion of the United States? Whipped Yankee Sullivan bare-fisted in thirty-eight rounds. And did you know he spent four years in the House of Representatives? One time Old Smoke offered to fight any ten Congressmen but no one took him up on it."

"Pity." Driscoll ordered a Black Russian and sipped it slowly.

"Sad thing is that none of it made any difference. Old Smoke spent his whole life trying to break into society and he never made it. No matter how much money he spent, people saw him as low class. Then he made the mistake of falling in with Cornelius Vanderbilt. There was a crook for you. He got Old Smoke to invest in railroads and Old Smoke lost a million dollars, dropped $800,000 on Black Friday alone. He died at forty-seven of a broken heart."

72

Driscoll stared silently into his glass.

"Bet you're curious why they called him Old Smoke."

"Ummm."

"Once when he was leading The Dead Rabbits, Old Smoke and another guy fought it out over a woman named Kate who ran a whorehouse. They did their fighting in a saloon. The other guy knocked Old Smoke into the fire, then sat on him until he started to burn. Well, Morrissey heaved so much that he threw the other guy off, but after that people always called him Old Smoke."

"So you aren't interested in Sam Cheney anymore?"

Charlie glanced at Driscoll. "Sure, but I heard he'd gone out west."

"I don't know anything about that, but I was talking to a young man who said he'd seen him." Driscoll went back to sipping his Black Russian.

"He saw Sam? When?"

"Recently."

"Who is this guy?"

"He's just someone who hangs around here sometimes."

"What's his name?"

Twisting uncomfortably on his stool, Driscoll said, "Tateo. He said he'd give me a call. You want to talk to him?"

"Sure."

They sat for a while without talking. Charlie didn't much like Driscoll and what he mostly didn't like was the way Driscoll looked: the long grey hair, the eyes too far apart, the way he dressed. Disliking these things, however, made Charlie friendlier than he might have been. He even went so far as to buy Driscoll another Black Russian. Driscoll accepted the drink without comment, and Charlie returned to his own thoughts which were mostly about Stacy.

At forty-one, Charlie still believed he could pick up any

new work and, depending on his effort, be successful. What depressed him about Stacy was that no amount of effort could make up for the differences between them. The fact that she was with Sam meant nothing. Even if she were unattached, it could never work. It was like a fish in love with a bird.

Driscoll was called to the telephone shortly after six o'clock. Charlie watched him talk for a few minutes, then nod, write something down and hang up.

When he came back, he said, "He wants you to go over and see him. It's only a couple of blocks."

"I thought I was supposed to talk to him on the phone."

Driscoll shook his head, then touched his hair to make sure he hadn't disturbed anything. "Some people don't like phones. He's at a hotel on Third Avenue. You know Hudsons? An army-navy store on Third and 13th? It's just north of there. Here, I'll draw you a map."

Charlie's feet hurt. He was certain he had walked twenty miles since coming to the city. But it was partly because he believed his feet shouldn't hurt, and partly because he didn't want Driscoll to think he disliked him, that he left The Lamplighter.

As Charlie was about to cross Second Avenue at 11th Street, a white Chevrolet pulled up beside him. Conrad Zack stuck his head out the side window. He looked at Charlie as if he were a specimen in a museum that didn't interest him much. Zack shook his head.

"Don't say I didn't warn you."

13

WHEN CHARLIE saw the hotel on Third Avenue, he guessed it did most of its business by the hour. It was called The Olympia and its narrow entrance was tucked between a pizza counter and a discount record store that blared music out onto the street.

Charlie went up a flight of stairs to a small lobby on the second floor. There was no one at the desk. The walls were a dirty pink and the pigeonholes above the desk were empty. Driscoll had told Charlie to look for Room 38 on the third floor. After waiting a little, Charlie continued up the stairs. There was no sound in the hotel.

Room 38 was down a short hall to the left of the stairs. Charlie knocked.

"Come on in."

Charlie opened the door, stepped forward and hesitated. It was a small room with green walls, a battered brown bureau and a double bed in a brown metal frame. The mattress was covered with a yellow bedspread. A lanky young man in blue jeans and a jean jacket was sitting on the bed. He had on dark glasses in thick black plastic frames. His brown hair was curly and clipped close to his head. Charlie thought he was about thirty, but it was difficult to tell because of the glasses.

"You Tateo?"

"That's right."

Charlie took another step into the room. Then someone gave him a slight push and the door shut behind him. Recovering his balance, Charlie turned quickly and saw a second young man who had been standing behind the door.

"Hi," the man said, and grinned.

He, too, was thin and wore jeans, along with a brown T-shirt. He had a small red stone in his right ear. It was more like a tie-tack than an earring. Charlie was mostly struck by his hair which was yellowish-orange. It was short and brushed back flat against his head, probably stuck down with something. It looked like cat's fur, an unhealthy cat.

"Nice of you to come," said the man.

Charlie guessed he was several years younger than the man on the bed.

"Why're you looking for Sammy?" asked Tateo.

"Because I want to find him."

Although Charlie now faced the bed, the second man remained behind him, so close that Charlie could feel his breath on the back of his neck. There were no windows in the small room.

"Yeah, but how come?"

"You know where he is?"

"He left town," said the man behind him. Charlie didn't turn.

"That's right," said Tateo. "He left town. How come you're looking for him?" The lenses of his dark glasses were moon-shaped, making Tateo's face look thinner and more delicate. He had almost no lips, just a horizontal line below his nose.

"Do you know where he went?" asked Charlie.

"Out west. He had to make a run."

76

"Run?"

"Hey, you a cop? We heard you're a cop."

"Saratoga Springs." Charlie considered giving Tateo one of his new calling cards.

"Shit, they got cops up there? Where's your horse?"

The man behind Charlie laughed; it was more of a giggle, an explosion of breath that tickled the back of Charlie's neck. He tried to ignore it.

"What d'you mean, he had to make a run?" Charlie asked.

"Just what I said. Sammy deals grass. He gets it in L.A. from a dude who brings it up the coast from Baja. So he goes out to L.A. coupla times a year, picks up a coupla kilos. No big thing."

"Why tell me? Why not tell Zack?"

"Zack?"

Charlie disliked talking to people who wore dark glasses. He also disliked men who wore earrings and dyed their hair. He disliked being breathed on, especially in a small, stuffy, windowless room.

"Zack's a narcotics lieutenant. He knows Sam. I saw him just this morning."

Tateo drew up his right leg and began picking at something on the heel of his boot. "If you're really down here because his mother's looking for him, why talk to Zack?"

"We're old chums."

Tateo stopped picking at his heel and slowly folded his arms. His jeans and blue denim jacket looked brand new. "You been talking to a lotta cops about Sammy?"

"Missing persons, and Zack of course. Did you see Sam leave for California?"

"That's what I been telling you, isn't it?"

"Did he drive, fly or take a bus?"

Tateo raised his voice. "How the fuck should I know.

What d'you think, I followed him? Maybe he flew. He didn't say."

"You want him to get busted?" asked Charlie.

There was another giggle from the man behind him. Tateo leaned back on the bed, supporting himself on his elbows.

"Sammy owes us some bread. I'm not worrying about that. If he gets busted, then this dude in L.A., he'll need someone else for his New York dealing. Right?"

"Sure." Charlie wanted to take his elbow and drive it backward. Instead, he decided to leave. "I guess that's that."

"You going back to your horses?" asked Tateo, sitting up.

"I expect so."

"Let him out, Jukes."

The man behind Charlie moved so that Charlie could open the door.

Once out on the street, Charlie decided not to go back to The Lamplighter. He would see if Stacy was home. He also wanted to think about Tateo and Jukes. He wasn't sure if he would mention them to Stacy.

WEDNESDAY

14

THE HEAT WENT ON in Room 931 shortly before six. By six-thirty it had climbed to over 100 and Charlie had been forced to open the window. The Puerto Rican maids began shouting at eight, and at 8:05 one of them simultaneously knocked on and opened Charlie's door. He slammed it shut. There were shouts of apology or at least he assumed it was apology.

Down the hall he could hear someone yelling, "Eight bucks, I pay eight bucks so I can sleep. What's this, a fuckin' jail?"

And a maid was yelling over and over: "No spika anglis!"

Charlie had read studies describing how prison guards became brutalized to the point where they thought the inmates no better than animals, and he wondered if a similar process was rampant among the maids at the YMCA.

Unable to return to sleep, Charlie lay on his back looking at the dirty white ceiling. He considered his dreams. A solitary man with many acquaintances, Charlie's dreams were filled with friends: people who didn't exist in a real world. Sleeping, he was always in a crowd, surrounded by men and women who felt kindly toward him. There were no celebrations or momentous events. His dreams had a pastoral quality, and whole nights might be spent picnicking or visiting friends or playing baseball. There was always lots of baseball, and once there had been a team of black bears in blue caps embroidered with the letter "B."

Occasionally, Charlie's wife would tell him her dreams and they would deal with fires and rapes, random violence, sexual frustration and insecurity—what Charlie thought of as working dreams. He felt himself lucky that his own dreams seemed to exist for the purpose of amusing him while he slept. That particular night he had dreamt of playing golf: as if his subconscious were attempting to deal with his sore legs.

It was later, during breakfast in the cafeteria, that the frustrations of the day began. The coffee tasted like plastic and had a reddish tinge. The cashier had been unable to give change for a twenty, and Charlie had had to wait until money could be brought from New Jersey or Connecticut, he wasn't sure which. The silverware, if it could be called that, was white plastic, and the knife snapped as he smeared grape jelly on his toast.

The cafeteria was a large room and each wall was painted a different color: red, blue, yellow and green. A sign on the blue wall said that occupancy by more than 201 persons was illegal. Although the cafeteria was half full, few people were eating. Again there was the split between young blacks and older whites down on their luck. These last sat together in small groups arguing passionately about tax rebates, subway fare hikes and the past. Two old men were ready to come to blows over whether Harry Truman had had a dog in the White House.

As he sat in the cafeteria, Charlie began thinking of Stacy. They had had dinner at an Italian restaurant a few blocks from her apartment. Although the food was expensive, customers were invited to take as much wine and antipasto as they wished. Consequently Charlie had gotten slightly drunk and gorged himself on greens in an attempt to bring down the general cost of the meal.

Stacy had talked about graduate school and how she hoped to work as a translator at the UN or some embassy. Her life was so different from Charlie's that he thought it like something he might read in a book. She was full of plans, the plans of someone embarking on her adult life, seemingly surrounded by alternatives. Charlie, in the middle of his adult life, could see the scarcity of his own alternatives and could anticipate what his next thirty years would be like.

Because of his growing infatuation, Charlie tried to find what Stacy said fresh and fascinating, but he could remember his own aspirations, and as a youth officer he had talked to many young people. In truth, he was slightly bored, and he began to take his interest not from her words, but from her beauty and youth. She had on a light green dress that looked expensive and her black hair was piled up on her head. The candle flickered light and shadow on her face, reflected from her green and slightly slanted eyes. The wine, the waiters speaking Italian, the flowers and dim light—all were romantic to the extent that Stacy became like an actress in a movie from Charlie's youth or some advertisement for expensive perfume or champagne. What was missing in Stacy's words was replaced by Charlie's memory.

But however much he might enjoy it, this too contributed to the foreign quality and seemed to stress their differences. Now and then, when he spoke of his own life and of being a policeman in Saratoga, he worried that she too might feel bored, but unlike him she couldn't take her pleasure from his face.

Charlie didn't mention Tateo or Jukes, nor did he talk

about Sam. It was as if he were separating her from Sam's world, pretending she wasn't involved. She didn't talk about Sam either, and her only reference to Charlie's presence in New York came when he walked her back to her apartment at nine so she could study.

They stood in front of her building and she took his hand. In the light from the streetlamp, Charlie couldn't help recalling similar occasions twenty years before when he had taken a girl home after a date. Stacy wore a long green and white striped scarf looped over her head and around her neck.

"I think you should go back to Saratoga," she said.

"Why?"

"It won't be good for either of us if you stay here."

"I don't plan to stay long. Will I see you tomorrow?"

"You should go back tomorrow."

At the time he had been flattered to think she was afraid of becoming emotionally involved. But sitting in the cafeteria of the YMCA, Charlie again saw her as part of Sam's world. After all, she had said they were both fives, and while Charlie didn't understand what that meant, it indicated where her loyalties lay.

At best their dinner had been a time-out period. More likely she had been looking for weak spots. As he thought that, he grew angry at himself for an apparent cynicism that belittled the strength of his feelings. But he had been a policeman for nearly twenty years. He knew the danger of letting down his guard, of thinking he was on vacation, of accepting the week as an extended birthday present.

Charlie didn't believe that Sam and Peter Bonenfant had gone to California. Alive or dead, he thought they were in New York, and he might have suspected dead if Stacy weren't so casual. He believed she was hiding something, but he doubted it was the death of her lover.

As for Bonenfant, Charlie wondered if Tateo and Jukes knew about him or if that mattered. He was aware their accusation that Sam was selling marijuana could easily be true. All that would stop Sam would be lack of opportunity. But again, Charlie didn't believe that Conrad Zack would involve himself over a few kilos of marijuana. Presumably he had perfectly competant subordinates to do that. He came back again to Peter Bonenfant. Charlie decided he wanted to know more about him.

Leaving the cafeteria, he checked at the desk and found a message to call Chief Peterson in Saratoga. This startled him. Although Peterson had okayed a week's leave, he hadn't known that Charlie was going to New York. His first impulse was not to call. Then he shrugged and walked toward the telephone room.

Charlie had worked with Peterson for over ten years. They weren't close but they respected each other. Charlie was a good youth officer, particularly skilled at handling runaways. Often he knew the kids from his contact with local organizations: Boy Scouts, YMCA, an orphanage, a variety of baseball teams.

Charlie's only complaint about his chief stemmed from Peterson's desire "to run a tight ship," which caused some paranoia within the department. Peterson had spent ten years in the military police and often spoke of them as the happiest years of his life. Charlie called him collect.

"Why didn't you tell me you were going down to New York?"

"I didn't see that it mattered."

"We've received a complaint. Doesn't that matter?" Peterson spoke in a gravelly voice which Charlie suspected he had copied from a policeman on television.

"Lieutenant Zack?"

"That's right. He says you're getting in his way. You

know as well as I do, Charlie, we gotta keep up relations with New York. Why're you looking for Sam Cheney anyhow?"

"His mother thinks something's happened to him."

"So what else is new? Coupla years in jail, it's just what he needs."

Charlie doubted that anyone would be better for a couple of years in jail. "I think something may have happened to him too."

"Look, Charlie, it's none of your business. Why the fuck didn't you just call? This Zack, he said he'd keep an eye out. What the hell can you do? No offense, Charlie, but you don't want to buck the NYPD. Do me a favor, come on back, will you? Zack said he'd call the moment he knew anything. You don't want to pick quarrels with cops."

Charlie found himself getting mad. Not at Peterson, who was caught in the middle, but at Zack. He saw Zack as behaving unfairly, of sneaking around behind his back. It dismissed him and seemed to show he wasn't worth bothering about, as if Charlie were some shadow person.

"Chief, I really think I'm on to something."

"Forget it, Charlie, it's none of your business. If you know anything just tell it to Zack and come on home. Okay?"

There was no point in angering Peterson. "Okay, there won't be any trouble."

"You coming back today?"

"Maybe not today. I've got some other stuff to do. Don't worry, I'll probably spend the whole day in a bar."

15

SOMEWHAT SENTIMENTALLY Charlie liked to tell himself that his earliest memory was his father's suicide. This wasn't quite true. What he remembered was that one day the house was full of large kindly men in blue uniforms who took care of him. He thought he remembered a gunshot, but he didn't. It was just that a shot was necessary before he could get to the more pleasant memory of the policemen.

Of his father he remembered nothing. His mother had had a snapshot, taken at a party, that Charlie had carried for years. It showed a room full of people eating, drinking and laughing while off to one side a small dark man was looking out the window. That was his father. He had wanted to be a jockey but he wasn't small enough for flat track racing. He had tried steeple chasing but had lost his nerve after breaking an arm. He disliked harness racing except for betting. "I should spend the exciting moments of my life looking into a horse's ass?" he had asked his wife. "It's too much like that already."

One day in early September when Charlie was four his father had come home and barricaded himself in an upstairs bedroom with a bottle of whiskey and an old Colt .45 automatic. Then, when the whiskey was gone and the police were forcing the door, he had shot himself. He left no note except for his IOU's. He owed the bookmakers about $25,000.

When Charlie got depressed, he would think of his father's suicide and remember the snapshot of the party and the man staring out of the window. But to cheer himself he would think of the kindly men in their blue uniforms.

Usually this led to a progression of memories: moving in with Uncle Frank, tagging along after his older cousins: James, Robert and Jack. Charlie had lived in his uncle's house off and on until he joined the army, although at least once a year his mother had rented a cheap apartment where they would stay until her money ran out. Hazel always did well in the summer and could count on steady work until Christmas. But by February or March, at a time when many waitresses went south, Hazel moved in again with her brother.

That morning at The Lamplighter Charlie was still brooding about his father's suicide when Lawrence A. Driscoll climbed onto the stool to his left. The interruption left Charlie in an unsettled frame of mind, and while he felt sorry for Driscoll, he barely saw him as among the living.

Driscoll sat without acknowledging Charlie, raising and lowering his grey eyebrows as if signalling to someone on the other side of the room. He still wore his green blazer, this time with a yellow shirt, and a tie with green and yellow flowers.

Charlie had come to The Lamplighter directly after talking to Chief Peterson since that was the place where people least wanted him to be. One of those people was Driscoll. Charlie assumed he was connected with Tateo and Jukes, but whether out of fear or money he didn't know. Probably both.

If Charlie had been looking for Sam in Saratoga, he would have talked to everyone who might have seen him and visited all the places he ever went. By sifting and re-sifting his information, he would have learned something. That was typical police procedure and what he was good at. But in New York it wasn't possible, and Charlie's only precedents came from films and fiction. He was a private investigator and his main clue was that he was disliked.

Although most people sometimes find themselves disliked, few take it as evidence of serious crime. Charlie was in the position of having to encourage his paranoia. Stacy wanted him gone, Zack wanted him gone, Driscoll-Tateo-Jukes wanted him gone; and Charlie felt that if he could make someone dislike him enough, then he might learn why.

"How's the free-lance consulting business going?" asked Charlie.

"I thought you might have returned to Saratoga."

Charlie tried to assume a jovial expression. "Not me. I've taken a lease on the stool. I've always had a soft spot for red vinyl. Fact I'm sitting on it. Ha! Those friends of yours, Tateo and Jukes, how'd you happen to meet?"

"I never told you they were friends," said Driscoll. There was a small gravy stain on the right lapel of his green blazer.

"Acquaintances then, what the hell. Buddies is buddies, right? Tateo and Jukes. What kind of names are those? Sounds like a vaudeville routine. 'I say, Jukes, I admire your guts.' 'Good heavens, Tateo, are they showing?' Then they do a little dance. Bet Tateo got called Potato as a kid. Probably soured him. You know them long?"

"Only a few weeks." Driscoll abruptly closed his mouth.

"That's what amazes me about this fast-paced world of ours. You know a man a few weeks and it seems you've known him your whole life. How'd you happen to meet?"

Driscoll glanced suspiciously at Charlie who was fiddling with an empty beer bottle.

"I don't know. They were in here one day and we just started talking."

"Where'd they come from?"

"Uptown, I think."

"Uptown? Oh, you mean in the city."

Charlie disliked being obnoxious. Like most people, he preferred to be thought well of, even by people he personally disliked. He decided to return the conversation to a friendlier level.

"You got a wife and family?" he asked.

Driscoll seemed slightly dismayed. "What do you mean?" He began patting and smoothing back his long grey hair.

"Just a friendly question. Lotta men have a wife and family, but, on the other hand, a lotta men don't, I guess."

"I was married once as a matter of fact," said Driscoll, giving Charlie a quick look. "It only lasted a couple of years. She wanted to go back to Philadelphia."

"Kids?"

"No."

"Me neither. Always regretted that. I even wanted to adopt one but the wife said no. Told me she didn't believe in taking care of someone else's mistakes."

Charlie paused. It seemed impossible to talk to Driscoll without sounding like a bumpkin. He decided to change the subject.

"So you're from Philadelphia, are you? Is that where you learned so much about locks?"

Driscoll quickly finished his drink as if preparing to leave. Charlie wondered if he had been in jail in Philadelphia. Molesting children? Exposing himself on buses?

Charlie doubted he had done anything as wholesome as robbing a bank. He found himself thinking of Stephen Arnold, a schoolteacher in Cooperstown, N.Y. In 1800 he had clubbed to death his six-year-old niece because she had been unable to spell the word "gig."

"I was brought up in Philadelphia, went to college there, then worked at Wanamakers. They transferred me to New York."

"What college?"

"Penn."

"Graduate?"

"Well, there was the war and. . . . Why are you asking me these questions? What business is it of yours?" Driscoll's ears began to grow red.

"Friendly questions, that's all, just friendly questions. I mean, it was Wanamakers in New York that used to be Stewart's department store, and it was Alexander T. Stewart who once owned the Grand Union Hotel in Saratoga where my mother worked. See how it fits together?"

As Charlie spoke, Driscoll got off his stool. His arms were pressed to his sides, but his hands jerked and fluttered as if caught in a small wind.

"I'm sick to death of Saratoga," he said.

"Then can I buy you another drink?"

But Driscoll was intent on leaving. "I'm sick to death of the whole business!" He turned and left the bar with more speed than Charlie would have thought possible.

Stacy appeared at three. If she was surprised to see Charlie, she didn't show it. She wore a short khaki skirt, a green sweater and her yellow jacket. As on the first time he had seen her, she was carrying books. Charlie couldn't make out the titles.

"I didn't know if you'd be here or not," she said. Her voice was friendly.

"What the hell, I've got the week off. No point in going back before I have to."

She smiled but didn't say anything. Charlie found it impossible to tell if the smile was sincere. He wanted her to like him, and couldn't bring himself to play the fool as he had done with Driscoll.

"Can I buy you a beer?" he asked.

"No, thanks, I've got a class soon. I just wanted to see if you were still around."

"Big and bold and full of the devil."

Stacy smiled again. "I meant to ask you, have you seen Zack again?"

"No, he just stopped by to say hello. Old chums. He likes the races in August." It hurt Charlie to lie. He wanted to tell her that Zack frightened him and that the policeman seemed to be having her watched.

"You don't plan to go back right away?"

"No, I'll stick around until Saturday. Take in a show or two. You want to have dinner tonight?"

"I can't. Perhaps I could meet you later."

"Here?"

"Sure. . . ." She began to say something else, and hesitated; balanced, it seemed, between several alternatives. Then she shifted the books in her arms, holding them tightly against her breast. "Well, I'll see you later."

As he watched her go, Charlie tried to guess what she had been about to say. Probably she had meant to urge him to leave. He hoped, however, that she had been about to refer to their dinner the previous evening: some memory that would have indicated the warmth of her feelings.

He thought again about the slight similarity between Stacy and Gladys, and wondered if that said something psychologically significant about Sam or merely about himself. He considered calling Gladys. It wouldn't have surprised him if she had heard from Sam. Charlie could see Sam frantically calling his mother, telling her he was fine and begging her to get that cop out of his hair.

It was fortunate that Gladys had lost all sexual attraction for him, but it was unfortunate that Sam had rejected all attempts at fatherly aid. Maybe that was sentimental. After her return to Saratoga, Gladys had continued her hints that Charlie was Sam's father. It was only later Charlie realized that these had begun at the same time as Sam's criminal career. They had even been effective. There were four or five occasions when Sam had avoided jail only because of Charlie.

Not that Sam had been grateful. In fact he had told Charlie to mind his own business. Nor had he responded to Charlie's attempts to get him interested in the Boy Scouts or baseball. Charlie had gone so far as to enroll Sam in a team composed entirely of boys rejected elsewhere, organized by some Rotarians who believed that every kid deserved the chance to play ball. One boy had been missing an arm, while another played from his wheelchair. Sam's only talent consisted of getting hit in the head by perfectly respectable pitches. At last one of the Rotarians had called Charlie, begging him to urge Sam to quit the team. Sam had needed no urging.

Gladys called Sam "delicate" and sometimes blamed his criminal career on being hit in the head with a baseball. Although she argued with passion, no judge had been convinced.

In his most logical moments, Charlie knew that his early affair with Gladys had been founded on hypocrisy. She hadn't really been interested in him. Rather she had been after his cousin, Jack, who was a year older and star tackle of the football team. But not only did Jack have clean tastes, he could get any girl he wanted.

Gladys would come over to the house, wait around for some sign from Jack and then go off with Charlie, maybe hoping to make Jack jealous. Jack never noticed. When Gladys finally accepted this, she dropped Charlie who was the team's assistant equipment manager.

Charlie had been crushed. For nearly a month he had hung around under Gladys' window at night, hoping she would see him and take him back. Then she had begun to tease him about being pregnant.

16

"WHATCHA COME BACK HERE FOR? Still think I'll show you that apartment? Fat fucking chance." Victor Plotz stood in his doorway, shading his eyes from the glare of the 200-watt bulb in the basement ceiling.

"Thought I'd come back for that other beer. How're the fish?"

"Those fuckers." Plotz turned and walked back into the room, leaving Charlie to close the door. "Got rid of the angelfish yesterday and today I find two dwarf gourami floating on the surface. Either the swordtail zapped them or they got flukes. Personally, I think they're suiciding. Bring 'em home, put 'em in a nice tank and zckzckzck," Plotz drew a finger across his throat, "they die. Never pick a fish for a friend. Fuckin' roaches are smarter. Beer's in the fridge, help yourself. Don't take the Heineken, I'm saving it for my birthday."

Charlie walked toward the kitchen. The cat, Moshe, jumped from the couch and followed him. "Did you give the angelfish to the cat?"

"I was going to, but I've had that fish five years. Was old enough to be the cat's mother, know what I mean? I told Moshe, I said, 'What d'you think, good fish grow on trees? Go chummy up to the Purina.' Nah, I gave it to a broad

95

upstairs. She's got a tank and said she'd let me visit it. Maybe it'll remember me. Who knows."

Charlie opened the refrigerator and took out a Rheingold. On the top shelf was a large blue bowl containing enough spaghetti for twenty people. Next to it was an old can of tomato juice with a cockroach perched on the rim. When it saw Charlie, it ran down the far side of the can.

"You know you got roaches in your refrigerator?"

"The bastards, as long as they don't touch the Heinekens, I don't care."

Charlie returned to the living room and sat down in the brown Naugahyde chair. Plotz stood in front of the aquarium scratching his elbows. His grey cardigan looked like a stray kindergarten class had been fighting over it. Along with the sweater, he wore wrinkled grey work pants and a white shirt. These were several sizes too large, as if Plotz had once been a much bigger man who had become smaller through some shock or loss.

The cat had followed Charlie back from the kitchen and was sitting by his feet. Charlie nudged it with his shoe. "I once knew a man who had mice in his refrigerator."

"Yeah?"

"Maybe just one mouse. It ate through a milk container, a full gallon, and all the milk poured down to the bottom of the refrigerator. Then the mouse fell in it and drowned. When the man opened the refrigerator, there was a great wave of milk with the dead mouse surfing on the crest of it."

"Guess I'm lucky, hunh?"

"Could be worse."

Victor sat down in the green chair. "Tell me, why'd you come back? Still hoping to see that apartment?"

"Will you let me in?"

"No can do."

Charlie looked down at the cat. It was motionless except

for the slight twitch of the eyelid over the empty socket. The twitch almost seemed a kind of teasing as if at any second the lid would spring open and reveal a tiny mirror or a painted scene entitled *Secrets of the Harem*. Charlie had once known a small boy at the Roman Catholic orphanage who had worn a glass eye that he used in playing marbles. Although the eye wasn't entirely round, it so unnerved the other players that their own marbles flew off in a variety of wrong directions.

"What I want," said Charlie, "is an address on that other guy, Peter Bonenfant. You said he'd been getting mail."

"Yeah, and he got a package today." Plotz leaned back and rubbed his bald scalp. He was pleased with himself. "Suppose you want to see the return address?"

"I'd appreciate it."

"They could get me for tampering with the mail."

"Look, Victor. . . ."

"Call me Vic."

"Okay, Vic, do me a favor before I kick in your fish tank, will you?"

"No need to get nasty. I'm just a fella, right? Gotta make a living same as the next man. You know I used to sell clothes? What I don't know about tweed suits you could put into a thimble. Wanna nother beer? I'll get it for you."

"Sure. Can I see the return address?"

"Sure, just hold your horses, will you? What's the fuckin' hurry?" Vic went out to the kitchen.

Moshe chose that moment to spring. Charlie caught the grey cat in mid-air. His eyes were watering. "I hate you," he whispered. Then he tossed Moshe toward the couch eight feet away. The cat landed on all fours and began washing itself.

The refrigerator door slammed shut. "Those fuckin' roaches, they want that tomato juice, they can have it. It's gone bad anyhow. You know you can kill roaches by putting out baking soda?"

Victor Plotz came back into the room carrying a Rheingold and a Heineken. He gave the Heineken to Charlie who appreciated the honor but accepted it without comment.

Victor returned to his chair. "The roaches eat the soda, see? Then they gotta belch, just like anyone else. Trouble is, they're physically unequipped to belch. The roach don't have a belcher. So instead of belching, he just gets bigger and bigger until Bang. He explodes. You put out a plate of soda and you hear this pop-popping all night long. 'Course after a while they stop eating it. I mean, roaches aren't dumb. They see their buddies turning to shrapnel before their eyes and after a while they wise up.

"So you try something else, like, for instance, Parmesan cheese. Roaches are crazy for Parmesan cheese. It's like whiskey, Jack Daniels, and they eat it until it kills them. You put out a little plate of Parmesan cheese before you go to bed and the next morning it's gone. But you know what? All around the plate will be a ring of fat little dead roaches all reeking of Parmesan cheese. Betcha could grind 'em up put 'em right on the spaghetti. Practically the same thing except for the color.

"Now me, I don't kill the roaches. 'Course if one's so stupid to fall into the tomato juice and drown, that's his tough luck. The owner, he has a guy come in and spray each month. That don't do much except piss 'em off. Betcha think I get so lonely that I keep roaches around to talk to. Them and the fish and Moshe. You wouldn't be half wrong. Bloop, bloop, that's all the fish do. Maybe it means something. Sometimes it gets so bad I go out and talk to the street light. It's the only fuckin' thing that won't walk away. You wanna nother beer?"

"Sure," said Charlie.

17

CHARLIE WAS A LITTLE DRUNK when he left Victor Plotz's apartment at eight o'clock, but in his pocket he had the name John Bonenfant and an address in San Diego. He guessed this was Peter Bonenfant's father. Charlie then went back to the Y to change his clothes, which were covered with cat fur, use the telephone and look for a place to eat. At the desk, he found a message to call his wife.

Charlie stared at it unhappily as he waited for the elevator. Marge, he was certain, meant to give him her good advice.

When Charlie unlocked his door he half-expected to find Zack on the other side of it. His room was empty. He hoped Zack had forgotten about him but knew that was unlikely. He felt like a mouse trying to make a cat disappear by wishing very hard.

Since he planned to meet Stacy, Charlie dressed carefully, putting on a pair of blue slacks and his last fresh shirt: a white Oxford cloth with thin blue stripes. Then he spent five minutes trying to decide on one of his three ties: blue with white horses' heads, red with yellow and orange stripes or green with white stripes. He regretted only bringing three and wondered what color tie he would have brought if he had known he was going to fall in love.

At last he decided on the horses' heads. He combed his hair, rubbed his shoes with a towel and took extra traveler's checks from his suitcase. He removed his .38, put it in a desk drawer, then changed his mind and put it on again, telling himself he felt uncomfortable without it. Having prepared himself for a possible lover, he went downstairs to call his wife.

Charlie had hoped Marge wouldn't be home, but she must have been waiting by the phone because she answered on the first ring. She went right to the point. "Charlie, Chief Peterson came by the store today. He said he'd received a complaint about you from the New York Police Department. What are you doing down there?" Her voice was like the high rat-tat of a child's drum.

Charlie made a face at the ceiling. An Oriental tourist looked at him suspiciously. "I told you, trying to help Sam Cheney out of another jam." He was irritated to discover that he was slurring his words. "How was your trip to New York? See some nice things?"

Marge ignored this. "Listen, Charlie, if I had a dime for every hour you've wasted on Sam Cheney. . . . Chief Peterson said your being in New York could make trouble for the department."

Their phone was in what Marge called "the television room," and in the background Charlie could hear the bright chatter and audience laughter of a variety show. "You know Peterson, he worries too much. I'll come home when I find Sam."

"Come home now. People have been asking about you."

They went back and forth. At last Charlie agreed to come home soon. He again felt angry with Zack for his interference and told himself he wouldn't return to Saratoga until he had finished his business in New York.

100

After hanging up, Charlie called San Diego information for John Bonenfant's number. When he dialed it, however, there was no answer.

By 9:30, Charlie had eaten and was on his way back to The Lamplighter. Afraid that he didn't have much time, he wanted to make as big a display of himself as possible.

Charlie found ten people at the bar and eight more in booths. Driscoll sat at the bottom of the U with an empty stool on either side of him. Charlie climbed onto the stool to his left.

"So how you been?" he asked.

Driscoll began to cough. The moving lights over the bar tinged his face red, blue and yellow, looking like emotions he was trying to repress.

"Sinus," said Charlie. "People always bothered by sinus this time of year. It's the pollen count. On the other hand, I once knew a man who choked to death on a piece of $10 steak. Want me to slap you on the back?"

"No, I'm all right now." There was a cringing look about Driscoll.

"You had me worried," said Charlie. He spoke loudly and saw people glancing at him. "Well," he continued, "it's a poor horse that won't drink water." He nudged Driscoll in the ribs. "I been celebrating. What the hell, you're only forty-one once. Hard life being a cop."

At the word "cop" Charlie saw Driscoll flinch. Several people at the bar turned toward him. Luke took some change and went over to the jukebox. Staring off to his right, Driscoll tried to pretend that Charlie was some complete stranger, a drunk who had just stumbled in.

Charlie glanced at the other nine people at the bar. Eight were men and any of them might be working for Zack. Mostly middle-aged, they were talking quietly or staring at nothing in particular. Sitting at the bar to Charlie's left was a woman about forty-five wearing an orange dress and thick orange lipstick. Her short black hair looked like a kind of bathing cap. On the bar in front of her were as least fifty colored beads which she was trying to string on a white thread. Her hand shook, however, and, as far as Charlie could tell, she was still on the first bead: a blue one that she held tightly between her left thumb and index finger. Her fingernails were painted to match her lipstick. Even she, thought Charlie, might be working for Zack.

Driscoll was still trying to ignore him. Charlie nudged him again in the ribs. "So when was the last time you were in Philly?"

Driscoll caught himself on the edge of the bar as the jukebox began booming out the Beachboys' *Good Vibrations*. "I wish you wouldn't do that," he said.

"Jeez, look, I'm sorry, hey?"

As had happened earlier, Charlie began to dislike being obnoxious. Although he would never choose Driscoll as a friend, neither did he wish him any harm.

"You ever play any ball?" he asked, trying simple conversation.

"Ball?"

"You know, you take a bat and a ball and maybe a good mitt . . ."

"As a matter of fact," said Driscoll, "I used to want to be a good first baseman more than anything, but they said I had flabby hands." He looked down at his hands as if they had tricked him.

"Oh, did you," said Charlie. He thought again of Salt Pork as Driscoll fussed with his tie, sipped his drink and appeared to regret the momentary confidence.

"By the way," said Driscoll, "that girl was in here earlier looking for you. What's her name?"

"Oh, her. Yeah, she's an old chum. The city's full of old

102

chums. What time did she come in?"

"About an hour ago. Isn't she a friend of Sam's?"

"Well, sure, she couldn't know me without knowing Sam."

Charlie distrusted Driscoll's interest in Stacy. He hoped he could make him leave before Stacy returned. "By the way," he asked, "have you seen your friends again?"

"Who do you mean?"

"Potato and Jukes: Five-foot-two-eyes-a-blue-kootchy-kootchy . . ."

"I told you, they're not friends of mine."

"When did you last see them?"

"Not for some time."

Driscoll's resistance seemed firm on that level. Charlie decided to try another tack. "You know, what I wouldn't give for a big glass of mineral water."

Driscoll raised his eyebrows. "Mineral water?"

"That's right," said Charlie. "Did you know that the first white man to take advantage of the springs in Saratoga was Sir William Johnson. He was suffering from the gout and rich living and some of his Indian buddies took him up for a cure. The Mohawks called the springs the Medical Springs of the Great Spirit.

"Sir William Johnson, there was a rogue for you. Spent nearly forty years living with the Indians. He'd a been hung in a white community. Every time he went on a visit, the Mohawks gave him a squaw to sleep with. It's a known fact that he fathered over 100 kids. The Mohawks, they adopted him and named him He-Who-Does-Much. Probably referring to those squaws . . ."

Driscoll climbed off his stool. "Excuse me," he said, "I have another appointment."

As he watched him go, Charlie tried to decide if Driscoll's questions about Stacy indicated an interest by

Tateo and Jukes. He considered telling her about the two men. To do so, however, would be to admit his continuing interest in Sam, which might change her from a friend and possible lover to a suspect and probable accessory.

Stacy appeared five minutes later. Seeing her, Charlie rediscovered a kind of erotic shyness that he hadn't felt for twenty years. In her yellow jacket, she looked like a brighter light come to compete with the ones over the bar.

"There you are," she said. "I stopped by earlier but you weren't here. I'm afraid I've got to do something right now. Will you wait? I'll be back by eleven."

She put her hand on his bare wrist. Charlie felt himself start. He disliked such Pavlovian reactions.

"I'll be here."

"You're sweet." She turned and left.

Sweetness and light, thought Charlie. He ordered another beer, and as he moved he became aware of the gun on his hip. It was an unpleasant reminder. He again told himself he was making a mistake to get involved with Stacy. But the warning was only a form of self-teasing which increased his growing excitement and his resolution not to spend another night on the couch.

It was now 10:15. To Charlie it seemed impossible that he could last out the hour with any semblance of calm. Perhaps he could name the banks robbed by Jesse James or the twenty-one men shot down by John Wesley Hardin. One of Hardin's victims had been a black policeman by the name of Green Paramoor. Charlie thought that was one of the most beautiful names he knew.

Maybe it would have been better three summers ago to let Sam go to jail, instead of giving him the chance to leave town. But it was years too late. Gladys should have put Sam up for adoption. She had always treated him more like a toy than a child. She and her sisters had the sort of rela-

104

tionship with their mother where she was only kind to them when they were pregnant or nursing. Gladys once told Charlie that he had nursed Sam, "till he'd just run up and grab it." She felt cheated that she only had one child, and envious of her two sisters who had seven illegitimate children between them.

Gladys' father had been a functional alcoholic who had worked at the stables. There had been two sons: one a mailman in Albany, the other in a mental hospital where he had been sent after it was discovered that what he liked best was burning down barns. He had destroyed twenty-five. Oddly enough, it was the mailman who was considered the black sheep, while the pyromaniac was seen as destined for riches. As Gladys said, "People will pay good money to keep you from burning down their barn."

Now, slatternly at forty-one, she specialized in obscure pains and fundamentalist religion, while worrying about her only son alone in New York.

She had not raised him well. Sam's most attractive trait was a childlike egoism that unfortunately kept his interest entirely on himself. An explorer within the boundaries of his skin, he was constantly searching for new ways to give himself pleasure. Charlie remembered a time when he had tried to teach Sam civic pride by taking him on a tour of Saratoga's mansions. Sam's interest had come from learning about the wealth of the original owners; his excitement from telling Charlie what he would do with an equal amount of money.

Sam had been arrested for stealing cars in 1965 and again in 1966. The second time he had been put on probation. He would have gone to jail if it weren't for Charlie. After he had told Sam what the juvenile home was like, Sam had stopped stealing cars.

Stacy reappeared exactly at eleven. She ordered a whiskey sour, which Charlie paid for, and they went over to a booth.

"Have you been having a nice vacation?" she asked. "What have you been doing?"

"Just wandering around." He wanted to tell her about Victor Plotz and his fish, but was afraid she would make fun of him.

"Wandering around where?"

"Times Square, Fifth Avenue, Central Park. My legs are killing me, but I enjoy it. I enjoy looking at things. You know they used to keep pigs and goats on 42nd Street? Used to be a real shanty town."

Stacy smiled. Her wide mouth reminded him of one of the star ballerinas who came to Saratoga each summer.

"It hasn't changed much," she said. She leaned forward with her elbows on the table. Her hair hung in a single black braid down her back.

"No? Maybe not."

"What kind of things do you look at?"

"Just things, little things. Like there was the window of a bookstore near Times Square. One of those pornography places? It was jammed with sex magazines and books. Lots of whips and rubber goods. But off to one side was a book of photographs called *Natural Childbirth Before Your Eyes*. Now that surprised me. Who would have thought it?"

Stacy reached out and took his hand. "Come back to my apartment," she said.

18

THE WEATHER had turned colder. Charlie buttoned his raincoat and pulled his hat firmly down to his ears. "I should have driven down here," he told Stacy as they walked up 11th Street. "If I was training for soccer, I couldn't do any more."

"It's just a few blocks," said Stacy.

"That's just the trouble, everything's a few blocks. It makes you feel foolish taking a bus."

They were alone on the street. Stacy walked a little ahead and Charlie had to hurry to stay with her. Their footsteps echoed off the buildings. Each time Stacy passed a gap between two parked cars, her stockings shone in the light from the streetlamp: small explosions of light.

"Bet there're rats around here," said Charlie. "Nice street like this, see 'em troop by carrying a baby or something."

While not drunk, neither was he sober. It felt like someone had spent the day stuffing cotton in his ears. Stacy continued to remain ahead of him. Apartment buildings and small shops on one side, parked cars on the other: Charlie felt as if he were being pulled along a narrow slide.

"What's the rush . . . ?"

As he hurried forward, Charlie heard a noise behind

him. He started to turn, but someone grabbed him, wrapping an arm around his neck and pulling him back. Then a second person stepped out from behind a Ford van. He wore a red ski mask.

Charlie twisted, trying to break away. The man in the red ski mask moved quickly toward Charlie and kicked out, his foot hitting Charlie's thigh and glancing into his groin. As Charlie retched, the man stepped forward and hit him in the stomach while the second man let go of his neck. Charlie fell to his knees, vomiting beer onto the sidewalk. For a second he remained resting on his knees and elbows, his forehead pressed against the cold vomit-smeared concrete. He was aware of a man on either side of him. He was aware of shoes: tennis shoes and boots. He couldn't get his breath and kept gagging. The pain in his testicles reached through each part of his body.

One of the boots moved out of Charlie's sight, then he felt a tremendous blow in his ribs. He rolled over, curling himself up. Before covering his head, he saw the other man, also in a ski mask: black with white vertical stripes that seemed to divide his face into slices. The man in the red ski mask raised a boot and kicked Charlie again. Charlie rolled in his vomit, trying to make himself smaller, guard his head with his hands.

As the two men started to kick him together, a horn began honking down the street. At first Charlie didn't hear it. Each kick made a small flash in his mind, blotting out all other sensations. But after a moment, the men stopped and Charlie heard the horn: quick, short blasts, over and over.

"Come on," said one man. "Get his wallet."

Charlie was aware of someone touching him. It was almost soothing. "He's got a gun."

"Take that too. Let's go."

The honking had stopped. Charlie heard their footsteps

running down the empty street. He lay motionless, feeling that if he moved he would shatter like a china cup.

He heard footsteps approaching. Afraid that the men were coming back, he tried to move but it was too awful. He thought if he could make himself as small as possible, then, when they kicked him, he would break like a milkweed pod and escape by floating away.

Someone touched his shoulder. "Chuck. Charlie."

Charlie didn't say anything. Pain filled him. There wasn't room for anything else.

"Charlie, I thought I could get help," said Stacy. "I was afraid. Can you get up?" Her voice was soft and concerned.

Charlie still didn't move.

Stacy knelt down next to him, stroking his hair. "Charlie, I'm sorry. Please say something. Should I get a doctor?"

Cautiously, Charlie tried moving. It hurt so he stopped. He could remember no time in his life when he hurt so much. He tried to speak but there was only a sound that cattle might make or a squeaky door. He could hear Stacy crying.

"Please, Charlie, say something. Are you all right? Please try to get up." She kept stroking his head.

He uncurled his legs and slowly rolled over on his back. There was a sharp pain in his left side and he guessed there was at least one broken rib, maybe more. He opened his eyes and saw Stacy in her yellow jacket kneeling beside him. There were tears on her cheek. Beyond her he saw a fire hydrant and a white Ford van parked at the curb. Light from the street lamp reflected dimly off a grey apartment building and grey fire escape. He could see the sky; there were no stars. He felt briefly that the sky was beneath him and he was about to fall.

"How badly are you hurt? Can you sit up? Let me help you."

There was more pain as he sat up. His hands slipped in the vomit and he fell back. Stacy took his arm and he got to his knees, then to his feet. He stood leaning against the Ford van, bent over with his hands on his knees. Slowly he straightened up. There was again the sharp pain in his left side. Stacy handed him his hat. It was crumpled but he put it on, half hoping it would help him think. He had never believed much in coincidences.

Stacy held his arm. "Can you walk? It's only a few blocks."

Charlie pulled away and nearly fell, slid along the cold metal of the van. "Leave me alone."

"Charlie, I . . ."

"Just leave me alone."

Whenever he spoke or breathed, there was another stab of pain. Charlie imagined his ribs red and burning. He was lucky they had stopped kicking when they did, that the horn had started honking.

Stacy moved back toward the apartment building. In the shadow, she became like a person disguised. "Charlie, you need help. Come back with me. It's not far."

Charlie shook his head. "I don't want to see you."

Stacy began to walk off, then turned back and took several steps toward Charlie, reaching out her hand so he could touch it if he wanted.

"Get away from me!"

Stacy turned sharply. Charlie watched her go, the yellow of her jacket beginning to blend with the dark. He leaned against the van, holding his sides.

"Stacy!"

She stopped about thirty feet away and stood with her back toward him. She looked small.

110

"Stacy, they took my wallet. I've no money to get back to the Y."

Slowly, she walked back to him, fumbling with her green Indian cloth bag and taking out her wallet. She gave Charlie a five-dollar bill. He looked at her with a great sense of loss. It was impossible to tell what she thought. Without a word or even glancing at him, she turned and walked away.

19

IT WAS PAST ONE when Charlie got back to the YMCA. He had stopped at an all-night restaurant and attempted to clean himself up in the men's room. His olive-green raincoat was torn up the back and smeared with vomit, reeked of vomit and beer. His blue slacks were torn at the knees. His shirt was torn and his blue tie had flecks of vomit between the white horses' heads. At his waist there was an uncomfortable feeling where his gun had been. The only identification he had left were the business cards he had bought on Tuesday.

In the restaurant had been a waiter immaculately dressed in a white jacket and black pants. He was Charlie's age, and even his general size and shape. He had stared at Charlie with such disgust, so obviously feeling that he should be taken out and drowned, that Charlie had lowered his head. The similarity between them was enough for it to seem he was staring at himself and that the disgust was his own.

If Charlie moved cautiously, his pains would subside into a series of aches, all except the pain in his left side. Entering the Y, he walked toward the elevators, careful not to look at the night clerk or the few people hanging around. He imagined the night clerk taking out his card and putting

112

a small check by his name.

It was when the elevator opened that Charlie remembered John Bonenfant in San Diego. At first he was tempted to forget about him. He didn't want to talk to anyone. He had already done enough for Gladys Cheney. But as he thought of his beating, he began to feel stubborn. The elevator door closed with Charlie still standing in the lobby. Certainly he would call.

A woman answered. Charlie asked to speak to John Bonenfant. Despite his bruises, he felt a slight thrill to be talking with someone who might be within sight of the Pacific Ocean.

"Hello? This is John Bonenfant." It was an older voice: educated and sure of itself.

"My name is Charles Bradshaw, and I'm with the Saratoga police department. Saratoga Springs, New York? And I'm calling . . ."

"Has anything happened to Peter?" The voice lost its sureness.

"Not that I know of."

"You startled me." He sounded relieved. "You see, we haven't been able to reach our son. Is there something I can help you with? I don't think I've ever been in Saratoga Springs."

Charlie wanted to hang up. He saw no way of not frightening this man in California. "Actually, I'm trying to find Sam Cheney."

"Then it is about Peter. I mean, Peter was staying with Sam. You say he's missing?"

"Not technically missing." Charlie tried to sound soothing. "We just don't know exactly where he is. Sam and your son probably went off someplace. You know kids. Probably decided to go trout fishing or something like that."

113

"Why are you looking for Sam?"

"Just wanted to ask him some questions. How did your son happen to come to New York?"

There was a pause. "Sam invited him. I thought it was foolish and that he should wait until August as he had planned . . ."

"Maybe you should tell me more about it. How did they happen to know each other?"

There was a crackling on the line. Charlie held tightly to the black receiver as if that pressure alone were holding up the wire to California.

"What sort of questions did you want to ask Sam?"

"Some of his friends are dealing marijuana," Charlie lied. "There may be trouble from outsiders."

"Trouble?"

"I don't want to talk about it on the phone, but anything you can tell me might be useful." There was a longer pause. Charlie pressed his head against the cool green wall. When he shut his eyes, he saw a figure in a red ski mask. "Are you still there?" he asked.

"I'm sorry. Peter was at UCLA and that's where he met Sam. I don't know the exact circumstances. Peter planned to go to graduate school in New York. NYU. He'd been accepted in psychology. But he meant to work this year and save some money. He was going to stay here until August, then move in with Sam until he found a place."

"What changed his mind?"

"Sam called around the beginning of March and told Peter that he'd found him a job. It was at the clothing store where Sam worked. He told Peter to come now and he'd lend him the plane fare. Peter had a construction job. He didn't like it much. So he decided to quit and go to New York. I thought he should stay. I mean once you start something . . . but, well, he quit anyway."

114

Dozens of telephone numbers were pencilled on the wall. Looking at them, Charlie thought it would have been kinder to call one at random than to call John Bonenfant.

"Did Sam ask him to do anything? Pick up anything for him? Go on any kind of errand?"

"As a matter of fact, he did. Sam asked him to pick up an envelope from a man in Los Angeles. How did you know?"

"Did Peter do it?"

"Yes, he picked it up the day he flew to New York. March 13. He really should have waited because it turned out the job at the clothing store fell through. I talked to him. He was having a good time, you know, sightseeing, but he said he'd have to start looking for a job right away. Since then we haven't been able to reach him. My wife keeps saying I should call the police. I was going to tomorrow. Don't you know anything?"

"No." Charlie again felt afraid for this man. "As I say, I only wanted to ask Sam some questions. His girlfriend told me he had gone out west."

"With Peter? But then he would have called. You think something's happened?"

"No, no, I'm sure they're fine. Kids is kids." There was nothing he could do to help John Bonenfant. Feeling like a coward, he slowly put the receiver back on the hook.

As he did so, he heard a faint voice saying, "Do you think I should call the police?"

20

CHARLIE FOUND ZACK lying on his bed reading *The Authentic Life of Billy, the Kid*. His black size-twelve wingtips were up on the green bedspread.

"Can't you be arrested for breaking in here?"

"Nope. How you feelin'?"

"How do you think?"

Zack put down the book. "Honking was all I could do. Anything else would have interfered too much."

"You could have driven down the street and made an arrest." Charlie took off his hat and torn raincoat. The smell of vomit sickened him. He sat down on the small chair by the desk and it creaked. "Get your feet off my bed."

Zack sat up and swung his feet around to the floor. He wore a grey overcoat, although the room was warm. "This is a delicate situation. You got no business . . ."

"Who were they?"

"Beats me."

"You're a liar. They got my revolver, you know that?"

"You shouldn't of been wearing it. Someday it'll be used to kill a cop and wind up on my desk."

"Break my heart."

Zack sat looking at him, elbows on his knees, holding his

116

grey fedora in his large pale hands. His grey crew cut was ragged, as if some large animal had been chewing on it. His face showed nothing except boredom. "They hurt you much?"

"Broken rib."

"You sure?"

" 'Course I'm sure. What'd you come down here for anyway? To gloat?"

It was difficult for Charlie to think that Conrad Zack had people who loved him. He imagined a yellow dog cowering in a cellar, waiting for its master's size-twelve footsteps. But presumably Zack had a more human side. Presumably there was a wife and children. He might be the kind of man whose eyes misted over at the thought of stray dogs and orphans, who enjoyed sitting around telling jokes with his pals who would know him by some affectionate nickname. After all, Jesse James was called Dingus by his closest friends. That had come about after the Centralia raid when Jesse had shot away the tip of his finger while cleaning his pistol. "If that ain't the dingus-dangast thing!" he had said. His brother Frank had called him Dingus from then on.

Even Alvin Karpis who had robbed banks with Ma Barker and her boys was called Old Creepy by Freddie Barker. Perhaps Zack was known by some name like Old Creepy.

Zack stood up and put on his hat. "If I catch you going back to that bar again, I'll charge you with obstruction."

"Why?"

"Because you're getting in my way."

Charlie slapped his hand down on the desk, making his toothbrush jump three inches and overturning a can of shaving cream. "You think I came to New York for a stupid reason? What right do you have to judge me? You go tiptoeing around, afraid I'm going to screw up some

117

narcotics deal of yours. I don't owe you a damn thing."

"How'd you know it's narcotics?"

"Since when's a narc been doing anything else?"

"How do you know I'm in narcotics?"

"Common knowledge."

"Stubborn prick, aren't you."

Charlie didn't answer him. Zack tossed his hat onto the bed and sat back down.

Two weeks ago we got a call from the San Francisco police. They had a woman in the hospital there. Two guys had broke into her apartment and beat her up, really took her apart. The police found some dope in her apartment, marijuana. They got a warrant and found almost a pound of it. That was on Thursday, March 20. The woman didn't want to talk at first, didn't want to get anybody mad. Then the police charged her with possession and she changed her mind. She said her boyfriend had a coupla kilos of pretty pure cocaine and that he was coming to New York to sell it. She said he was going to make the sale this Friday."

"Who beat her up?" asked Charlie.

"Dunno. But apparently the boyfriend was doing the run for someone else. Then he got greedy and decided to keep the whole thing for himself. These two guys, they're probably working for the other guy, the one that owns the dope."

"And it's coming to The Lamplighter?"

"Not necessarily, although the woman in California knew the name of the place. Actually, the boyfriend had set up a mailbox in New York where he'd pick up any last-minute information. We got the mailbox staked out. But The Lamplighter's involved and if you keep hanging around the whole deal might be cancelled. We can probably get all kinds of information from this guy, but we can't do anything unless we bust him with the dope."

118

"You think Sam Cheney's going to buy it?"

"Beats me."

"What if I don't go back?"

Instead of answering, Zack reached over and picked up the book on Billy the Kid. He began leafing through it. "You know this book of yours, there's a sentence here that made me think of you. 'His misfortune was, he could not and would not stay whipped.' Ring any bells? I'm not kidding about that obstruction charge. You hang around that bar and I'll throw your ass in jail."

Zack put on his hat and stood up. "Come on, I know a man who'll tape up those ribs."

"Don't do me any favors."

"Come on, come on, don't be a twerp."

Charlie got to his feet.

THURSDAY

21

THE NEXT MORNING Charlie awoke before the arrival of the Puerto Rican maids. His bruises and the pain in his side made sleeping impossible. He lay on his back and stared at the picture over his bed showing the Maine coast and the man pulling the red rowboat out of the water. It occurred to Charlie that he knew nothing of the criminal history of Maine.

Along with his discomfort, he felt keenly frustrated. What had begun as an attempt to make his life more interesting had gotten out of control. Charlie had seen himself as coming to New York City, finding Sam Cheney and returning to Saratoga a modest but definite hero. Because of Zack, however, he must return having failed. He thought of Zack's threat to arrest him for obstruction if he went back to The Lamplighter. He knew Zack wasn't lying. What Charlie minded most was Zack's refusal to obey the rules of Charlie's own fantasy.

At least Zack had begun to treat him more as an equal. Not that they were friendly, but Zack seemed to accept Charlie's silence about his beating as a kind of stoicism. That was fortunate because Charlie was angry enough to ignore Zack's warnings if he felt he weren't being taken seriously. Perhaps Zack had seen that. Stubbornness is a form of passivity, and like many quiet people Charlie could be extremely stubborn.

They hadn't talked much when Zack had driven him to a police doctor. Charlie could see that Zack was being kind, as far as he was able, and felt guilty at not having done more to stop Charlie's attackers.

The police doctor had found three cracked ribs. He had taped him up and told him to avoid physical activity.

"Cracked?" said Zack. "Shit, you said they were broken."

By the time the Puerto Rican maids began their shouting, Charlie had decided to return to Saratoga. That was a pity. For years he had believed himself content, but after three days in New York he found himself questioning the fabric of his life: his job, his wife, his three cousins.

He was not yet discontented. He was still interested in his life. But he was surprised at how willing he was to shed those things he thought he valued. As he got out of bed, he wondered what it would matter if he never went back to Saratoga. He thought of his friends and acquaintances. Despite the little he knew of Victor Plotz, there was no one in Saratoga he would set above him. As for his wife, Charlie only had to review his willingness to get involved with Stacy to make him question the value of his marriage.

Marge was an important object, rather than a person. That was the role she had chosen, and it made her as much a part of his life as his house or car or job. In a way, Charlie didn't mind that. He always knew who she was. Marge never had doubts or questions, and Charlie, who was always questioning, was comforted by her certainty while often disagreeing with her conclusions. But there wasn't much emotion in their marriage. As for their house, it was a ranch house in a newer part of town. They lived there because Marge said it was easy to clean. Charlie thought the same could be said of a paper bag.

Beyond Zack, there was another reason for returning to Saratoga. He was embarrassed by how easily he had been manipulated by Stacy. And even now, when he was sure she had used him, he was afraid he would let himself be used again if he didn't leave the city, which, after all, was what she wanted.

When he went downstairs, Charlie found a message to call Chief Peterson in Saratoga Springs. As he read it, he told himself he should rip it up. There was nothing Peterson could say which would encourage Charlie to leave now that he had reached that decision for himself. Therefore it was almost out of perversity that he went into the telephone room.

He got through to Peterson right away.

"Charlie, that New York lieutenant called me again yesterday afternoon. What the fuck you doing down there? He said if you don't leave, he'll pick you up for obstruction. Charlie, this can only mean trouble for one person."

There were six phones in the phone room and three others were occupied by men calling about jobs. Charlie cupped his hand over the mouthpiece. "What do you mean?"

"Charlie, the papers would have a field day with this. If you got arrested in New York, what d'you think we'd look like? Jesus, Charlie, are you trying to ruin us? Twenty years or no twenty years, if you're not up here today I'll have to suspend you. This Zack, he even said you'd found yourself a little chippy. What about Marge? You gotta good woman there, Charlie. You musta gone right round the bend."

Charlie had the sense that Peterson was a stranger, someone he was talking to for the first time. "I want to find Sam Cheney. He's in trouble."

"Look, Charlie, you're the one in trouble. I mean, I don't care if a dozen chinks are feeding him ground glass. I told you, if you're not in my office this afternoon, you're out. There'd have to be a hearing, but I'd hope you'd have the decency to resign. You know as well as I do, Charlie, these things can be a can of worms."

What bothered Charlie most was Peterson's assumption that he had no reason, purpose or justification for being in New York. He imagined Peterson sitting in his office with its paneling and black leather. Peterson raised show dogs: Irish setters. On the walls of his office were framed color photographs of his three champions seen from a variety of angles, plus citations, awards and bits of parchment commending him for raising the quality of the breed.

"I don't mind telling you, Charlie, this Zack, he scared me. We talked some. He almost went so far to say that if you didn't get back up here, he'd cut us off. Look, Charlie, you know what that means. This year we're going to have the biggest fair in the whole state. Two fucking weeks. And the trots start next Thursday. We depend on New York. There are times if they hadn't tipped us, we'd of looked like fools. Drugs, pickpockets, you know that as well as I do. Where would we be if they didn't call us? Even one summer? Some smart crook come up here, we'd look like clowns. So tell me, what are you going to do?"

"You'd really suspend me?"

Peterson snorted. "What fuckin' choice do I have? They pick you up and the reporters get it and the wire services, the fuckin' papers up here would be fighting for it. Television, radio, it'd be a zoo, Charlie. One of my men arrested for obstruction? A sergeant? My hands would be tied. At best, I'd have to say you were sick, that you'd gone off your fuckin' rocker and I'd had to let you go. What else could I do? What the fuck, Charlie, you know what

126

life's like. You gonna be in my office today?"

Charlie put his hand against the wall and pushed slightly. "Sure," he said, "I'll be there."

"That's a promise, right?"

"There's a bus at eleven."

"Hey, Charlie, check in with me. Okay? We'll have a coupla laughs over a beer."

"Sure. Sure thing."

Charlie went upstairs to pack his bag.

22

CHARLIE WAS A MAN who liked eating and enjoyed cooking. As he walked up Ninth Avenue toward Port Authority Bus Terminal, it was an indication of his frame of mind that he could pass so many stores dedicated to food with such apparent lack of interest.

Although his mind seemed blank, he was aware that some part of it was thinking and would not be distracted by stores specializing in nuts, spices, tea and coffee, fruits and vegetables. The only exception was a butcher shop. Hanging in a row in its window was a white rabbit, a black rabbit, a grey rabbit and a small pink pig. Charlie had never eaten rabbit. His sensibilities would not allow him to eat an animal that, deep down, he still referred to as "bunny." But, pausing before the shop window, he wondered if there was any difference in taste between white, black and grey rabbit.

He hurried on. Although this Thursday was the most spring-like day of his visit, Charlie was freezing. He had left his olive-green raincoat wadded up in a ball in a YMCA wastebasket. Torn and smelling of beer and vomit, the coat would only make people stare. His grey sport coat, however, although wool, was too thin to be effective. It seemed unfair to Charlie that along with his bruises and disappoint-

128

ments, he should be cold as well.

He reached the bus station shortly before ten. Learning that an Adirondack Trailways bus left from Gate 27 at eleven o'clock, he went down to the lower concourse to wait. The terminal was crowded, and Charlie moved slowly because of his ribs, trying to avoid being bumped into. Across from Gate 27 was a row of plastic seats. He lowered himself into the nearest.

He felt dissatisfied with himself and betrayed by the people around him. It seemed he had spent his whole life following the instructions of others, and that even now he was leaving his self-appointed task because that was what other people wanted.

Charlie knew if he stayed in New York, he faced arrest and the loss of his job; more than his job, his whole life in Saratoga Springs. But what now bothered him was the feeling that his life in Saratoga wasn't very important. Indeed, one of his reasons for returning was to convince himself that he was wrong, that he was perfectly happy with his life as policeman, husband, cousin and all-around good guy. And he would have gone readily if there weren't such pressure on him to go.

Charlie felt increasingly defiant The more he was pushed, the more he wanted to find Sam Cheney. He also felt that if he found Sam, then he would be free of him, as if Sam were an irksome spirit who had inhabited him for twenty-five years. To find him would be to exorcise him.

From the moment he had learned Gladys was pregnant, Charlie had thought of the child as his. It wasn't until fifteen years later that he discovered that was impossible. He was sterile. After five childless years of marriage, he had forced himself to see a doctor, submitted to tests and learned he could never father a child.

Sam Cheney was not his son. But after thinking him his

129

son for fifteen years, and listening to Gladys' coy hints that he was Sam's father, it was difficult not to feel fatherly. Sam might be no good, but he was as close to a son as Charlie would ever have.

Perhaps that was why Gladys found him so easy to manipulate. Charlie had always wanted a large family. He had seen himself as living in a large Victorian house surrounded by children of all sizes. When he learned he was sterile he felt as if someone had died.

He regretted not having children. He knew he was the sort of man who would take great pleasure in organizing a child's birthday party: renting a Hoot Gibson movie, buying horns, hats and inviting twenty-five guests. He would even force it on the shy child who was terrified of parties and would suffer through the celebration.

Childless, Charlie tried to content himself with orphanages, the children's wards of hospitals, various baseball organizations. He became known as an easy touch by the more enterprising children of Saratoga. The Girl Scout cookies of one year would last into the next. Young salesmen of greeting cards, candy, magazines would put Charlie at the top of their list, while children with seeds would walk across town to sell him the parsnip and turnip seeds that no one else wanted, even though Charlie planted nothing but a few tomatoes.

Charlie was a man of fatherly feelings and many of them had been directed toward Sam. But along with these feelings, he had a very clear idea of what Sam was like. Charlie hadn't come to New York with any thought of rescuing an innocent child from a den of vipers. More likely it would be the vipers that needed rescuing. But he still wanted to find Sam.

He assumed that Sam and Peter Bonenfant were hiding in the city, waiting for the cocaine. Jukes and Tateo were

130

also waiting for the cocaine. The sale was to take place on Friday. What was one day? Charlie told himself he was leaving too soon.

Sitting in the bus station, he knew his life had reached a place of major choices. He could stay in New York or he could return to Saratoga and continue his life as a youth officer. But, although that was what he was best at, there would be no surprises. He could anticipate almost everything that would happen until he retired.

Charlie guessed that another factor pressing him to leave was his own fear. He was frightened of Zack. He was frightened of being beaten again. He was frightened of losing what he had achieved in Saratoga. But his fear embarrassed him. His decision to go or stay seemed a matter of morality, and he felt it wrong to be influenced by physical fear and economics.

Charlie found himself thinking of Black-Face Charley Bryant, a member of the Dalton Gang, who had once boasted, "I want to get killed in one hell-firing minute of smoking action." He had had his wish, dying in a gunfight with a U.S. Marshal whom he mortally wounded.

Even better were the last words of Billie Clanton as he lay in the dust of Fremont Street near the O.K. Corral. Wounded five times and with Wyatt Earp standing over him, Clanton had raised his empty pistol and said, "God, God, won't somebody give me some cartridges for a last shot."

As further encouragement, there were the words of Wyatt Earp himself as he raised his guns at the beginning of that shoot-out: "You sons-of-bitches, you have been looking for a fight and now you can have it."

It was 10:40. Gate 27 was about fifteen feet away. The lower concourse was actually a sloping corridor, about thirty-five feet across and 100 yards long. One end was about twenty feet higher than the other, so that a bowling ball released at the top to Charlie's left would create havoc when it reached the coffee shop called—Charlie craned his neck—*Post and Coach Snacks* thirty yards to his right. Next to the coffee shop was a flight of stairs leading to the main concourse and the Eighth Avenue Subway. A policeman stood by the stairs.

Seeing him, it occurred to Charlie that the man had been sent to make sure he got on the bus. That was improbable. If Zack sent anyone, it would be a plainclothesman. But once he had thought it, Charlie was certain he was being watched. He began to get mad. It was wrong of Zack to hound him.

At no point did Charlie think that Zack's problems were any concern of his. Nor was he leaving because he thought that to stay would interfere with the course of justice. He might want to find Sam, but he wouldn't protect him from arrest if that was what he deserved.

Charlie wondered why Tateo told him that Sam had flown to California. And he wondered why he hadn't mentioned Peter Bonenfant. Perhaps he didn't know about him. Altogether, Charlie found Bonenfant's involvement curious. He had brought an envelope from Los Angeles to New York which presumably contained part of the money for the cocaine. But although Bonenfant might have been an innocent courier, Charlie couldn't imagine him hiding with Sam, waiting for the sale on Friday.

It then occurred to him that Sam and Peter Bonenfant might not be together. It was plausible they were together but not necessarily true. But if they were apart, where was Peter Bonenfant? As he thought this, Charlie had a great desire to see Sam's apartment.

A speaker in the ceiling announced that the Adirondack Trailways bus to Albany, Saratoga Springs, Glens Falls,

132

Lake George and Warrensburg was now receiving passengers. Charlie picked up his bag, walked toward the gate and joined the few people who were gathered in line. He glanced around the lower concourse for someone who looked like a plainclothesman. He could see about 100 people and any one of them might be working for Zack.

At the head of the line, the Trailways driver was stamping tickets. Charlie recognized him as the same man who had driven him down three days before. That time seemed long enough to be measured in years. The driver took his ticket; he didn't recognize Charlie. The door gave on to an open area where the buses were parked; beyond them were lanes by which they entered and left the building.

As he passed through the door, Charlie very calmly told himself that he wasn't going back to Saratoga. He walked toward the bus until its bulk hid him from the windows of the lower concourse, then he ducked down and moved toward the exit lane. Turning left, he jogged up the ramp, staying close to the darkness of the far wall. With each running step, there was a spurt of pain from his side. He still carried his suitcase and it banged against his knee. A few drivers and porters stared, but made no move to stop him.

When he got outside, Charlie paused to catch his breath and reaccustom his eyes to the sunlight. He thought of Black-Face Charley Bryant. Walking toward Eighth Avenue, he began looking for a bank where he could cash his traveler's checks and a liquor store where he could buy a large bottle of Jack Daniels.

23

"YOU'RE BACK, are you? Didn't figure to see you again."

Victor Plotz held open his door. His dust-kitty hair was mussed and Charlie guessed he had been sleeping. Hibernation would be more like it. With his size and shambling gait, he seemed related to a Walt Disney bear.

"Brought you a present." Charlie handed Victor a brown paper bag.

Victor drew out the bottle of Jack Daniels. "You must wanta see that room pretty bad."

Putting down his suitcase, Charlie passed through the living room into the kitchen. Moshe jumped off the couch and followed him, weaving in between Charlie's legs. Charlie took a tray of ice from the refrigerator and knocked it into a blue bowl. Then he found a couple of glasses and returned to the living room, still followed by the cat.

Victor stood by the suitcase with his hands pushed down in the pockets of his grey cardigan. He had opened the whiskey and put it on the table by the fish tank.

"You want the glass that says, *Peanut Butter Can Be Fun*," asked Charlie, "or the one with Bozo the Clown?"

"Long as it holds whiskey, what's the diff? How come you brought a suitcase? You a slow drinker?"

"I was going back to Saratoga, then changed my mind. Can I leave it here for a while?"

Victor took the Bozo the Clown glass, put in two ice cubes and filled it half full of Jack Daniels. "Sure, sleep on the couch if you want. What the hell. You okay? You look a little peaked."

Charlie sat down on the brown Naugahyde chair. The question made his bruises ache. "Some guys beat me up last night, trying to get me to leave. They took my wallet and revolver. I lost all my ID. There wasn't much money in the wallet, but the revolver, that's embarrassing. You're not supposed to lose your revolver. Also, I'll have to pay for a new one."

It occurred to Charlie that he wouldn't be needing a revolver if he were fired, nor would he be needing his new business cards.

"The bastards. They hurt you much?"

"Not much," said Charlie. "How're the fish?" Looking toward the tank, he noticed some new vegetation and that the orange diver was gone.

Holding Moshe, Victor sat down in the other Naugahyde chair and began scratching the cat under its chin. "I finally discovered the guilty party. It wasn't the angelfish after all. It was the fuckin' swordtail, the red one. I caught him bustin' a guppy. Too bad, the swordtails were always Moshe's favorite. Sometimes they'd get excited and jump out of the tank. I'd find 'em lying between Moshe's paws. Moshe didn't hurt 'em or anything, just licked 'em very, very gently. Fuckin' fish practically had a stroke. Didn't jump out of the tank for a while, I can tell you. But bustin' guppies, that's something else again."

"What'd you do?" asked Charlie. He imagined Moshe in a black hood and holding a headsman's ax.

"Had a regular trial. Put the swordtail in a glass in front

135

of the tank, put Moshe up on the table, then put the last surviving guppy in a glass on the other side of him. You know, the grieving widow. No question that the swordtail was guilty. I mean, I saw him with my own eyes. Had a regular execution, just like Sing Sing. Zap. Gave the swordtail to Moshe right in front of the tank as a warning to the other fish. No licking this time. Coupla quick bites and he was gone.

"Anyway, I been making some changes. Got rid of the diver which I figured was riling them up. Bought some more green veg, Ludwigia it's called. And from now on I'm raising nothin' but mollies: nice peaceful fish that don't eat their kids and don't mind dirty water. Just toss in some salt and you're all set. The molly is God's gift to the lazy man. They'll even eat lettuce in a pinch."

The cat jumped off Victor's lap, wandered over to Charlie and sat down by his feet. Trying to ignore it, Charlie glanced around the room. There was an old portable television on a table by the couch. On top of the television was a stack of crossword puzzle magazines.

"How long have you lived here?" Charlie asked.

Victor finished his whiskey. "Seven years last February. Had a place in Brooklyn but when Matt, he's my son, when Matt moved to Chicago I said, what the fuck I need five rooms for? And I heard about this job and, well, everything worked out." He looked around the room and his eyes settled on the fish tank. "It's good for the fish. Basements are naturally damp."

"What happened to your wife?"

"She died thirteen years ago. Cancer."

"I'm sorry." Charlie thought with self-dislike that his idea of conversation had always been to ask questions. Out of shyness and a fear of silence, he was constantly prying into other people's lives.

136

"Not your fault, nor mine either. That's one good thing about cancer. You can't blame me for it." Victor got up, put several more ice cubes in his glass and filled it half full.

"You're not drinking enough," he told Charlie. "How you going to get me drunk if you're not going to drink yourself? Sarah, that was my wife, she never appreciated good drinking. And Herbie Schultz, he didn't either. They would have made a fine couple. Schultz owned the clothing store where I worked. He was always kissing ass. You know, an Italian to the Italians, a Jew to the Jews. He never even voted 'cause he was afraid of being caught picking a side. Stores like that, they're like mastodons. It specialized in middle-aged Jewish men. The dumb fuck. Times change, that's all. That's what pissed me off about that friend of yours, Sam Cheney. Works in a clothing store, does he? He don't know the first fucking thing. He'd make jokes about us being in the same business. I spit on him. Ah, what the hell, it's a living, right? What's it matter what a man does as long as he washes his hands. Take you, for instance, a cop. You musta seen a lot of stuff. Does it show? You got the face of a baby. I'm not making fun, don't get me wrong. You always been a cop?"

By two o'clock the Jack Daniels was nearly gone. Charlie had been trying to hold back, but he had drunk almost a third. The conversation had continued to be about their own lives, bringing up one event after another as if they were mathematicians going over columns of figures to discover how certain sums had been reached.

At one point Charlie found himself saying: "My mother, she's always had this idea that she's about to become rich. Either she's going to marry a Vanderbilt or one of her trotters is going to turn out to be Secretariat or something. And you know what she's going to do with the money? I remember as a kid, we'd be living with my uncle; and my mother, she'd always be talking about opening a tourist home. She'd spend whole evenings just describing it. Over the years I got to know that imaginary house better'n any place in Saratoga. It was going to be a big three-story white frame house with a screened-in porch on three sides and two wineglass elms in the front yard. And there'd be a green sign with the word *Guests* painted in white, and the name of the house: Happy Haven or Wayfarers Arms, she could never decide which. But she'd talk about that house until you could hear the creak of the glider on the front porch.

"It'd cater to people who came for the races: gentlemen of the turf, she'd call them. Flats by day, trots by night. And each year the same ones would come back and she'd always have free ice and papers.

"Then the elms died and motels got big, and she started thinking of having a motel instead, something small, no more'n twenty units, and she'd call it Shady Nook or Bidawee and again the same gentlemen would come back year after year and think it was good luck to stay there, and there'd be free ice and papers. Every time a new motel went up in Saratoga, she'd get mad because that was just where she'd meant to have her own."

"You know those people?" asked Victor. "Like the Vanderbilts?"

"Sure, I mean they come up in the summer. And the Whitneys. They come up too. That always sort of irritates me. People call Saratoga a one-month town. I live there all year round." Charlie paused as Victor poured the last of the Jack Daniels into his Bozo the Clown glass. "Say, Victor . . ."

"Vic."

"Okay, Vic, say you walk into the john and find $50 on the floor, and then, say, I walk into the john and find a key lying on the floor and say this key just happens to be the one to Sam Cheney's apartment. Then say I go out for a little walk and I come back and you just happen to go back to the john and, what the hell, you must of dropped your keys because there they are lying right on the floor and you pick 'em up and put 'em in your pocket and nobody knows a thing. What d'you think about that?"

Victor got up and walked to his desk. As he bent over, rummaging through the belly drawer, he looked like half an arch made of soft grey stone. After a brief search, he took out a ring with two keys. He tossed the keys to Charlie who caught them in his right hand.

"You want those keys so much, then you can have them. I'm not takin' money from a buddy. But if the landlord hears about it and I lose my job, then I'm coming up to Saratoga with Moshe and the fish and pester you til' you find me another. Okay?"

Charlie put the keys in his pocket. "Sure. I even know of an opening on the police force."

"I don't know about that," said Victor, "it doesn't need to be anything special. Just talk to those Vanderbilts of yours. But since you have all that money and since we're out of Jack Daniels, you might consider contributing ten bucks toward another bottle. What d'you say?"

"Sure," said Charlie, drawing out the money.

24

THE 9x12 LIGHT GREY RUG was filthy and spotted with crumbs, cigarette butts and three empty Genessee bottles, but between the two windows that looked out onto 6th Street was a lighter patch that had been recently cleaned. Charlie knelt down beside it.

It was an area shaped like a horse's head, about four square feet and next to the yellow linoleum between the rug and the wall. Part of the linoleum had also been cleaned. Lifting the edge of the rug, Charlie saw that the clean linoleum extended beneath it, following the general shape of the horse's head. On the underside of the rug, however, was a brown stain. Charlie was almost relieved to see it.

Taking out his pen knife, he scraped the stain, then looked at the brown flecks that had come off on the blade. He wiped the blade on the rug, and inserted it between the floor and molding. Scraping it back and forth several times, he saw there were new brown flecks on the blade. Charlie stood up and inspected the knife in the sunlight. The brown flecks took on a reddish tinge.

Putting his knife away, Charlie crossed to a green couch along the opposite wall and sat down. The apartment reminded him of Sam: pale, shabby and secretive. It was a studio apartment: one room, 15 x 20, and a kitchenette closed off by a grey plastic shower curtain. Charlie had earlier made the mistake of looking behind it. The dishes in the sink had been spotted with mold and cockroaches. Grease and tomato sauce had been caked on the white enamel of the two-burner stove.

Sam's room was furnished with a Murphy bed, a green couch, a bureau and a seemingly brand-new pink formica table and four metal chairs with padded seats and pink vinyl backs. Charlie couldn't imagine Sam buying them.

The two windows had venetian blinds but no curtains. Between them was a poster for a New York Dolls concert. On the wall above the couch was an Escher print of a bunch of geese turning into a bunch of fish or vice versa.

As he looked around the apartment, Charlie wondered how much he would care if Sam were dead. He knew he would regret it. His second thought was that he would hate to break the news to Gladys. There was a photograph of Gladys on the bureau next to a small pile of *Mad* magazines and *Playboy*. The photograph was a grainy 8 x 10 enlargement of the sort of snapshot taken by machines in dime stores. It showed Gladys at age twenty laughing and looking up to her left, probably toward the young man who was paying. Her forehead was hidden by bangs and her blond hair curled just past her shoulders. Even at that age she had begun to look seedy: bad teeth, poor complexion. Her lipstick was crooked and smeared.

It occurred to Charlie that Sam's father was probably Louie Farelli who now sold cars in Glens Falls. Louie had about a dozen illegitimate children scattered across Saratoga, Washington and Warren counties. He had been two years ahead of Charlie in school. When Gladys had begun to publicize her pregnancy, Louie had left town, returning only after Gladys had gone to Warrensburg.

Charlie had last seen Louie Farelli at a veterans meeting in the fall. He had gained forty pounds and lost his curly black hair. During the evening, he had told Charlie three times that his doctor had made him give up Scotch and Vichy.

Charlie began to search the apartment leisurely, pulling down the Murphy bed, going through the drawers of the bureau, looking in the closet. He had hoped to find a picture of Stacy but there wasn't one. Although he inspected all the clothes, he didn't think there were enough for two people.

The bathroom was filthy. There was a stall shower with a torn green curtain. The mirror over the sink was flecked with toothpaste. Around the rim of the white toilet seat someone had written, "Dis is de place," in black ink. There were no towels and only one toothbrush.

Charlie wanted to talk to Driscoll and Stacy. He knew they had lied to him, but he wasn't sure of the importance of what they had concealed. He decided to see Stacy first. Perhaps he could learn more about Bonenfant. As he went downstairs to return the keys, he wondered what would happen when Zack discovered that Sam had had a roommate.

Charlie found Victor stretched out on the couch with his eyes closed, and singing, *I'll give you a daisy a day*. The cat had disappeared and the fish were behind the Ludwigia. On the floor next to Victor was another bottle of Jack Daniels about two-thirds full. Charlie put the keys on the desk and left quietly.

25

EITHER STACY wasn't at home or she refused to answer her bell. It was 3:30 so she could easily be at NYU. As he walked away from her building toward the Bon Marché store on the corner, it occurred to Charlie that Zack might be having her building watched.

He knew he should be paying more attention to Zack, but, having decided to ignore him, he was making the mistake of forgetting about him as well. Zack could arrest him, and would certainly arrest him if he had known Charlie was on his way to The Lamplighter. But Charlie doubted that Zack was searching for him. The policeman probably assumed he was on his way back to Saratoga. Not that he had any evidence of that, but Zack was used to being obeyed and might substitute an assumption of obedience for proof.

The sky was cloudless, although hazy, and the day had become warmer. Charlie was almost comfortable in his sport coat. When he neared Astor Place, he began looking for a cab. He knew if he approached The Lamplighter on foot, he would most likely be stopped; but if he appeared in a cab and went directly inside, he hoped he would be safe. Since Zack was trying to watch the bar unobtrusively, he wouldn't have Charlie dragged out.

Briefly, Charlie wondered how he would get away again. That could be dealt with later. Although he knew Zack was serious, it was difficult for Charlie to believe him. Without any tangible threat, his conflict with Zack became a sort of game, an involved version of Capture the Flag. But even as he thought that, Charlie was aware of his error: that his rules came from his own fantasy. He was like the bettor who confidently puts $10 on the 30-to-1 shot simply because he wants that horse to win.

In any case, his desire to talk to Driscoll was greater than his fear of Zack. Charlie now saw himself as searching for Bonenfant rather than Sam. Driscoll had never mentioned Bonenfant. Either he didn't know about him or he was hiding something. But it seemed unlikely that the Driscoll-Tateo-Jukes faction knew nothing of Bonenfant, especially since it was Bonenfant who had picked up the money in California. If possible, Charlie wanted to get Driscoll away from the bar, take him someplace where he could exert more pressure. Maybe he could rent an uncomfortable wooden chair, a gooseneck lamp and a 200-watt bulb.

There were five customers in The Lamplighter and Driscoll wasn't one of them. They didn't look up when Charlie entered. He imagined they were all plainclothesmen. Taking a cup of coffee, five Slim Jims and a bag of chips over to a booth, Charlie sat down to wait. He asked himself if he would be acting this extravagantly if he hadn't drunk so much Jack Daniels.

Charlie's tangible threat from Zack came ten minutes later. He had gone to the restroom and was standing at the urinal. As Charlie unzipped his fly, a man entered and went up to the urinal beside him.

144

"Want some good advice?" said the man.

Charlie disliked conversations at urinals, especially with strangers. "What?" he asked. He didn't look at the man but at a graffito which warned him that if he was reading this message, he must be pissing in his shoe.

"You get out of here right now and maybe you'll only get yelled at. You hang around here and you'll go to jail. Zack, he's ready to kill you."

As he zipped up his fly, Charlie tried to think of some cutting answer. The man was Charlie's age and wore greasy blue coveralls. Charlie had seen him before and had assumed he repaired Jaguars. There were even spots of grease on his face.

"You must really want to go to jail," said the man. "You self-destructive types, what d'you get out of it?"

This time Charlie shrugged. But walking back to his booth, he had an impulse to leave. He dismissed it. Whatever the consequences, he had made his decision. Now he needed to figure out how to get Driscoll out of The Lamplighter without Zack's interference.

Driscoll appeared at 4:45. He tried to show no surprise at seeing Charlie. He still wore his green blazer, this time with a yellow shirt and plain purple tie. Charlie realized that Driscoll wore it not out of fondness but poverty, and he guessed that free-lance consulting was not one of nature's money-makers. Seeing that Driscoll intended to avoid him, Charlie called him over.

"Say, Mr. Driscoll, I believe I owe you an apology. Sometimes when I been drinking a little, I let my tongue run away with me and, well, you know how it is. Can I buy you a drink?"

At first Driscoll looked suspicious, but Charlie's apology required acknowledgment. Charlie saw several more food stains on Driscoll's blazer, and thinking of Salt Pork he

145

imagined this quiet man experiencing his only passion when confronted with a plate of spaghetti.

"Perhaps a very small one."

"What'll it be?"

"Perhaps a Black Russian." He lowered himself slowly onto the seat across from Charlie as if he suspected the booth to be a kind of Venus's-flytrap. On the wall above the two men was a theater poster advertising Lauren Bacall in *Applause*.

When Charlie returned with the Black Russian, he found Driscoll more composed. "Have you been sightseeing?" asked Driscoll.

Charlie sat down across from him. "More or less. Did you know that Bowery is from a Dutch word meaning farm?"

"You don't say." Driscoll sipped his drink.

"Actually," continued Charlie, "I'm in a lot of trouble. Never rains but it pours. Right?"

"How do you mean?"

"The police are looking for me."

Driscoll leaned forward as if he thought he hadn't heard correctly. "What on earth for?"

"Well, you see, I let myself get carried away when I was looking for Sam. I broke into his apartment. The super there, a guy named Plotz, he called the police this morning."

"What are you going to do?" Driscoll's composure had disappeared.

"Get out of town, I guess. Trouble is I'll probably be picked up at the bus station. If I could get over to Paramus, I'd be all set. The bus to Saratoga stops there after it leaves New York. I don't know, whatever happens I'll be in hot water. The cops will probably bust in here and arrest me."

"In here?"

"Why not?"

146

Driscoll leaned back in the booth and looked at his watch. It was five o'clock. With his square head and thick grey hair combed back, his face became a series of rectangles. Charlie imagined his photograph under the caption: *Can you draw this man? A career in commercial art can be yours.* He tried to decide if a student could capture the worried expression and slight trace of fear.

"But you're a policeman," said Driscoll at last.

Charlie laughed. "That doesn't mean anything. Sure, the New York cops will call Saratoga, but my chief doesn't even know I'm down here. I told him I was sick. When he learns I'm here, he'll be furious. He'll probably tell the New York cops to keep me. You know, throw away the key?"

Driscoll nodded in a depressed sort of way. Charlie glanced toward the bar and saw the pretend mechanic in his greasy coveralls staring at him. He decided to give Driscoll another push.

"I got a plan though," said Charlie. "When the cops pick me up, I'll tell them that I think something happened to Sam. Maybe he got killed."

"But that wouldn't be true. What would you do that for?"

"Law of the jungle. Dog eat dog. Can I buy you another drink?"

Driscoll shook his head. He fidgeted with his empty glass, rattling the ice cubes. "What if I drove you to Paramus. I can get a car. At least I think I can."

"That'd be swell," said Charlie. "You're a good buddy."

Driscoll winced as he got out of the booth. "Let me make a call."

147

26

DRISCOLL HAD GONE to get a car. The plan was for him to drive up to the back door of The Lamplighter at exactly six o'clock. Charlie would jump into the back seat and be driven away. He didn't entirely like the plan, but everytime he tried to think of another he noticed the pretend mechanic watching him from the bar. At least it would thwart Zack. He saw himself as disappearing from beneath the policeman's nose, and took pleasure in imagining his anger. Looking at his watch, Charlie saw he had twenty minutes to wait.

There were now about thirty people in the bar. Most had come in since five and about half were retired men allowing themselves their first drink of the day. At the back of the room, four young men were doing their best to break the Foos Ball game. Occasionally a ball would go skittering across the floor and the smallest of the four men would chase it, followed by shouts of "There goes Joe" and "Go get 'em, Joe." The jukebox blared out the Pointer Sisters. Charlie continued to drink coffee.

Driscoll had told him to expect a grey Valiant. Charlie was to get into the back and lie down on the floor. Driscoll would then drive to Paramus, or at least that was the plan. But Charlie meant to find out more about Peter Bonenfant,

148

and he meant to find out more about Tateo and Jukes, who were certainly the ones that had beaten up the woman in San Francisco. It seemed he could get that information without the extreme step of going to New Jersey.

Charlie disliked waiting. Twice he had called Stacy but there had been no answer. Sitting in the booth, it was too easy to doubt the wisdom of his plans; and he worried that he might have fallen into a losers' syndrome he had experienced at the track: that the more you lose, the more you bet in hope of making up your losses.

What was he throwing away and for what reason? As Charlie waited, it seemed that his main reason was pride, that having decided to find Sam Cheney he would do it no matter what the cost. With mild astonishment, Charlie wondered at the series of events that had led him to jeopardize all that he thought important; but with that astonishment was some pleasure that he refused to be controlled by the circumstances of his life.

The Cousins would never understand that. Charlie tried to guess what they would say when they learned he had been suspended. Or worse: that he was in jail in New York City. He could see them shaking their heads and offering to lend him a little money. They wouldn't be terribly surprised. James, five years older than Charlie, was a carpenter and owned a small construction company. Robert, three years older than Charlie, sold insurance and real estate. Jack, a year older, managed a hardware store.

The Cousins were men who never felt temptation. Their lives were as orderly as a bus trip. Apparently content, they couldn't understand Charlie's mild restlessness.

For years, they had told him he was the luckiest man alive: good job, lovely wife, lots of friends. What more could he ask for? And Charlie, although he didn't want more, felt guilty that he wasn't happier, that he would daydream about sneaking off to, say, Elkhart, Indiana, where he would get a job with the fire department and live a life almost exactly the same as his life in Saratoga Springs. He found it frightening that as he got older there seemed fewer opportunities, that he could anticipate a future without surprises.

At one minute to six, Charlie left the booth and walked slowly toward the back door of The Lamplighter, just past the rest rooms. His hat was still on the table, and he was careful not to look at the pretend mechanic. At six exactly, he opened the door. There was the grey Valiant. The engine was running and its rear door was open. Charlie half-dove and half-fell through it, trying not to bang his ribs. The Valiant started forward and the door slammed shut. The sudden motion made it hard to keep his balance as he knelt on the floor. The car turned quickly out of the alley onto 10th Street, and Charlie was pushed down onto his left shoulder. He was surprised by the smell of perfume, then he felt something cold brush his cheek. Managing to turn over, he looked up into an automatic pistol less than an inch from his eye.

"Didn't expect to see me, did you?"

Charlie caught a glimpse of yellow-orange hair before the gun was shoved against his eyelid, forcing him back down to the floor.

"You know," said Jukes, "you shoot a guy in the eye like this and it hardly makes any noise at all. The dude's whole head acts like a kind of silencer. I heard once that you can do the same thing by cramming an apple onto the barrel. Trouble is, I don't have any apples."

"You're not going to kill him?" asked Driscoll. He sounded terrified.

"No, you dumb fuck, I'm just going to put out his eye. Why don't you watch out where you're driving. Hate to have an accident with me half over the seat like this."

150

27

IN JOHN WESLEY HARDIN's account of his capture by Texas Ranger Lieutenant John B. Armstrong on
the train in Pensacola in 1877, Hardin said that when
Armstrong placed his pistol against his forehead, he told
the lieutenant, "Blow away! You will never blow a more
innocent man's brains out, or one that will care less!"

Further, that when Armstrong's men began to pound on
John Wesley Hardin with their gun butts, Armstrong
stopped them, saying, "Men, we have him now; don't hurt
him; he is too brave to kill and the first man that shoots
him I'll kill him."

Charlie tried to draw comfort from this as he was forced
up the stairs to Driscoll's apartment. Jukes had one hand
on his collar while shoving his pistol into Charlie's right
ear. The pistol hurt. Driscoll led the way, but kept turning
around as if to make sure Charlie was still alive.

Unfortunately, Armstrong's own account differed too
much to allow Charlie to take solace from Hardin's. Armstrong said that as he walked down the aisle, Hardin recognized him as a Texas Ranger and attempted to stand up
and draw his guns at the same time. He moved too quickly,
however, and his guns caught on his suspenders. As Armstrong described it: "He almost pulled his breeches over

151

his head." Armstrong then stepped forward and cold-
cocked him.

Tateo was waiting in Driscoll's apartment. He wore dark
glasses even though the shades were drawn. He had on new
blue jeans and a jean jacket.

"Have any trouble?"

"Clockwork."

"Did he have a gun?"

Jukes shook his head. "Some cop he is, right? Maybe up
in Saratoga the cops carry cattle prods or something." He
slapped Charlie on the back, making him stumble forward.

It was a shabby apartment, and Charlie doubted that
Driscoll had changed anything since first coming to New
York. There was a dark-panelled hall, then the large living
room with a purple rug and purple drapes obscuring the
windows. The two armchairs and couch were Germanic
and rectangular. A design of dark flowers and ivy ran in
vertical stripes on the greying wallpaper.

Tateo sat in a low purple armchair, facing Charlie with
his feet stretched out in front of him. His brown cowboy
boots had high heels and pointed toes. Above him was a
black metal birdcage on a black metal stand. The cage was
empty.

"What are you going to do with him?" asked Driscoll.
He stood back in the hallway, holding his hands crossed in
front of him. It made him look like someone come to in-
quire about a job. He was careful not to look at Charlie.

Jukes grinned at him. "Don't worry. Whatever we do,
we'll do someplace else."

He and Charlie stood in the center of the room, his gun
resting lightly on Charlie's ear. It acted like something
electric on Charlie's mind, kept him from concentrating.

Tateo raised his right hand and pointed a finger at
Driscoll. "Go get a necktie." He spoke quietly, almost in a
whisper.

152

"Will I get it back?"

"No."

Driscoll moved out of the hallway toward a door on the left side of the room. He walked quickly as if barely keeping himself from running.

Jukes tapped Charlie's ear with his gun. "Lie down on the floor. Face down."

Charlie got down slowly. He had bumped his ribs in the car and it was painful to move. The purple rug smelled musty. He watched Driscoll return, or rather he watched his brown shoes. Beyond him, in the other room, he saw a brown wooden bedstead.

"This tie all right?"

"S'long as it ties, what the fuck?" Jukes prodded Charlie with his shoe. "Okay, Saratoga, put your hands behind your back."

Charlie did as he was told. He felt the tie wrapped around his wrists, and winced as it was pulled tight.

"There," said Jukes, "I wasn't in the fuckin' Boy Scouts for nothing." He walked over to a dark green couch and sat down. Driscoll continued to stand at the bedroom door, as if he thought he'd be less at fault if he remained partly out of the room.

For a moment, Charlie lay quietly, then he rolled over. He would have sat up but he couldn't because of his ribs.

"Hey, Saratoga, I didn't say you could do that."

"Leave him alone," said Tateo. He hadn't moved since Charlie had been brought in. Charlie guessed he was staring at him, but he couldn't be certain because of the dark glasses. With their thick plastic frames and moon-shaped lenses, they seemed to cover half of his thin face.

"What'd you tell the cops about us?" asked Tateo.

"Nothing."

Tateo turned toward Jukes who got up again and walked over to Charlie. "I asked you a question," said Tateo. He was still almost whispering.

"I told you, I didn't tell them anything."

Jukes raised his foot. Charlie tried to twist away but he wasn't fast enough. Jukes kicked him in the shoulder, and Charlie rolled over groaning.

"I mean it," said Charlie, "I didn't tell them anything."

Jukes followed him, kicking him lightly in the back. "Hey, Driscoll, you want to kick him this time?"

"Of course not."

"Don't be a lily-ass, kick him in the face."

Driscoll stayed in the bedroom doorway. "No, please, you said I didn't have to do anything."

"Sit down, Jukes."

Jukes grinned and walked back to the couch. He wore jeans, tennis shoes and a black sweatshirt with the sleeves cut off at the shoulders. In his right hand, he carried a small black automatic. Charlie didn't recognize the make. Turning quickly, Jukes tried to spin it in a border roll but the pistol was too small. He raised it, grabbing his wrist with his left hand, and swept the room in a wide arc. "Bepbepbepbepbepbepbepbep." He laughed, then sat back down on the couch. "So what we going to do?"

"I already told you." Tateo still faced Charlie.

"All that way? I though you were joking."

"No."

"That's a fuckin' stupid idea."

Half sitting up, Tateo turned toward Jukes. He didn't say anything, just stared until Jukes began to grin.

"We're taking him to see Sammy," said Tateo at last. "That's the way I want to do it."

Jukes shrugged, then raised his pistol and again swept the room in an arc. "Bepbepbepbepbep. You like my gun?" he asked Charlie. "Tateo gave it to me. Iron. That's what they say. 'He's packing iron.' " He grinned.

Charlie was struck by how much his yellowish-orange hair looked like fur: dyed rat or weasel, short and plastered back on his head. He again noticed the red tie-tack earring.

"Tateo collects guns," continued Jukes. "This one's Italian. A Beretta 9mm automatic pistol Model 1934. Right, Tateo? Takes a .38 shell. They used 'em in the Italian army. It's got RE stamped on the grip. I don't know what that means. Maybe *real effective*. Is that what it means, Tateo? Bepbepbepbepbepbep."

Charlie lay on his side watching Jukes. He felt sick in his stomach but he didn't intend to give them the pleasure of seeing his fear.

"Did you two beat me up last night?" he asked.

Jukes lowered the Beretta. "Us? When?"

"Last night about 11:30. I'd been at The Lamplighter. Some guys beat me up and took my wallet."

"No fooling. Wasn't us, Saratoga. I don't approve of beating guys up. It's a good way to fuck up your hands. I mean, if you want to get a guy, why not just shoot him? You might as well go whole hog. Don't get me wrong, I know guys that swear by it. But to my way of thinking, nothin' beats a pill in the eye."

Charlie thought of the girl who had been beaten up in San Francisco.

"They hurt you much?" asked Jukes, as he again tried to do the border roll with the Beretta.

"Cracked some ribs."

"No fooling. First that happens and now this, right? Guy never knows when he's well off. Who do you think they were?"

"Junkies."

"Wouldn't be surprised. What a way to fuck up your life."

Charlie didn't answer. He lay quietly, trying to keep his

155

fear from overwhelming his mind. Jukes kept playing with his pistol; Driscoll fidgeted in the doorway. Only Tateo seemed motionless. He still faced Charlie with his sharp-toed boots stretched out in front of him. He could have been made out of wax. Charlie imagined the eyes moving behind the dark glasses.

"Let's go," said Tateo. "It's dark enough."

Along with his fear, Charlie felt hopeless. There were no alternatives or compromise. He thought of the bodies he had seen as a policeman: homicides, accident victims, suicides. He thought of his own body, lying in the careless manner of the dead, surrounded by a small ring of officials who shuffled their feet, spoke quietly and had seen it before. He strained to pull his wrists apart but the necktie wouldn't give.

Jukes stood above him. "Okay, Saratoga, get up."

Charlie rolled over on his stomach, got to his knees, then to his feet. "Where we going?"

"Tateo's got this plan to take you over to New Jersey."

"Shut up."

"It's a fucking stupid plan, Tateo!" shouted Jukes.

Tateo stood up and took a step toward Jukes.

"Okay, okay," said Jukes, "but why take him so far?"

Tateo spoke softly. "Because that's what I want to do."

"But why?"

"I just told you." He turned away.

Jukes grabbed Charlie's arm and pulled him toward the door. "What can you do with a guy like that?"

There was a noise from Driscoll. He started to move toward Charlie, then stopped. His face became wrinkled. "I . . ." He didn't say anything else.

"You lily-ass," said Jukes. Letting go of Charlie, he

156

stepped forward and hit Driscoll in the stomach. It was like a dancing exercise. Driscoll twisted away and fell back against the wall, holding onto his stomach as if it had broken in his hands. He slid down the wall to the floor.

"There," said Jukes. "If you hit a guy, hit him where he's soft. Just watch out for his belt buckle, that's all."

"Come on," said Tateo. "Stop fucking around."

As Charlie was taken down to the car, with Jukes' pistol again pressed to his ear, he searched his mind for some comforting recollection. But the only person he could think of was Cherokee Bill who was hanged in Oklahoma Territory in 1896 at the age of twenty for killing thirteen men. As he was led to the gallows, he looked up at the sun and blue sky, and said, "This is about as good a day as any to die."

When the guard asked him if he had anything else to say, Cherokee Bill answered, "No. I came here to die, not make a speech."

28

THEY WERE GOING through the Lincoln Tunnel. Tateo drove. Charlie sat beside him, twisted uncomfortably to the left because of his tied hands. Jukes, perched on the edge of the back seat, rested the muzzle of his Beretta lightly against Charlie's jaw. Grey sponge rubber dice with pink spots hung from the rear view mirror. Attached to the top of the steering wheel was a clear plastic knob containing a small yellow rose.

"How'd you know Sammy was going to deal cocaine?" asked Jukes, giving the pistol a slight push.

Charlie tried to raise his head away from it. "He told me. He was trying to raise the money to buy it. He said it was an investment. Whatever I put in, he'd double."

"Did you do it?"

"I didn't have the money right then."

"Jeez, fine fucking cop you are."

"The stuff belong to you?"

"Belongs to a man we work for."

It was hard for Charlie to believe that he was being taken someplace to be shot. Jukes seemed perfectly calm, was simply indulging in a little light conversation with a fellow passenger. Tateo, on the other hand, ignored them completely. He had removed his dark glasses, but Charlie still

158

couldn't see his eyes. He thought of a time several years before when he had been given the dubious honor of holding a young boa constrictor. Charlie had been amazed by its muscularity. Looking at Tateo, he imagined him like that boa constrictor, while, without the dark glasses, Charlie expected to see small, black pebble eyes. It frightened him more than Jukes' Beretta.

"Why bother about me?" he asked Jukes. Charlie couldn't bring himself to say the words "kill" or "murder" or "shoot."

Jukes kept his pistol against Charlie's jaw. "It's easier, that's all. You shouldn't of been hanging around that bar. I mean, it's not as if we don't like you or anything. You're not a bad guy."

"Thanks," said Charlie.

"Now me, I wanted to do it in the city, but Tateo thinks different. He likes everything neat and orderly. What the hell, we go a little out of our way, who's going to regret it?"

They had left the Lincoln Tunnel and were driving west on Route 3. "Where are we going?" asked Charlie.

"Tateo once worked out here, driving a truck. What's the name of the place? Secaucus, that's it, Secaucus. Sounds like a bird, don't it?"

"Why don't you shut up, Jukes." Tateo spoke without turning his head.

"What the fuck, who's he going to tell? Sammy?" Jukes gave a high laugh, then leaned forward and whispered in Tateo's ear. Charlie couldn't hear what he said.

Jukes sat back again, giving Charlie's head a slight tap with his pistol. "To my way of thinking, any delay is another chance taken. A bird in the hand, you know? Not that I mind driving around, don't get me wrong. This is my first visit to the City and so far I like it a lot better than L.A., although we haven't exactly been sightseeing. But I'll come back, you don't have to worry about that. When I see a place I like, I always come back. Like Mexico City. Remember that, Tateo? Shit, did we have one fuckin' time."

Tateo didn't say anything. He had turned south off Route 3. There wasn't much traffic, but occasionally another car would pass in the opposite direction, lighting up their faces and making the sponge rubber dice glitter. On Tateo's face, the light looked like a mask, stressing the sharp angles of the nose and jaw. On either side of the road were chain link fences and corrugated metal warehouses. The land seemed swampy and wet.

"It don't look like much," said Jukes, "but where we're going you can even see the Empire State Building."

Tateo slowed down and turned right on a narrow paved road. With each turn, Charlie became more afraid. He knew his main hope depended on appearing calm, of convincing Jukes that he wouldn't cause trouble. It seemed that he and Jukes were acting out some dangerous hypocrisy in which both pretended that nothing of any importance was about to happen. Charlie decided to carry his bravado a little further.

"Look, guys, I wonder if I could ask you a favor, for my wife's sake."

Jukes gave the pistol a shove. "What's on your mind?"

"My wife, she's squeamish, I mean, things bother her more than most people, so I wonder, you know, when you shoot me maybe you won't do it in the face. It's going to be bad enough on her just to do the ID." Charlie felt some satisfaction at the control he had over his voice.

Jukes was silent for a moment. "You're a hard little fucker, Saratoga, I gotta say that for you. Sure, you give us no trouble and we'll keep you pretty. Promise?"

The grey Valiant crossed a single railway line, then Tateo turned right onto a narrow dirt road that followed the

160

tracks. The headlights swept across high reeds. Charlie thought it was about ten o'clock. He didn't answer Jukes. After driving about 100 yards, Tateo stopped and turned out the lights.

"Get out of the car."

Jukes quickly opened his door and got out while keeping his gun against Charlie's head. He unlocked Charlie's door and opened it. "Come on," he said.

Charlie got out of the car. He was embarrassed to discover that his legs felt weak. Tateo came around the front holding a small flashlight. He shone the light briefly in Charlie's face, then turned it toward a path. "Let's go."

Jukes didn't move. "Tateo, what's the point of taking all these chances? Let's do it here."

Tateo took a few steps along the path, then stopped. He didn't turn around. "I'm going to let him see Sammy."

"What the fuck's it matter? I mean, in ten minutes it'll be all the same. If some watchman calls the cops, Jesus, Tateo, it's not worth it."

Moving quickly, Tateo came back to Jukes, stopping a few inches from him. He didn't speak or touch him, but just stood facing him for about fifteen seconds. Again Charlie was reminded of the boa constrictor. At last Tateo turned and walked up the path, shining his light a little behind him so Charlie could follow.

Jukes grabbed Charlie's arm and shoved him along the path. "You ever seen someone with a cut throat, Saratoga? A big double grin? Your wife, she sees that and she'll puke. Believe me. You just walk along behind Tateo and keep quiet."

Charlie followed Tateo along the path. He felt almost grateful to him for keeping him alive, and he was relieved to discover they were afraid of making noise. The path was muddy and at places it was covered by an inch or so of

161

water. Tateo's boots left bullet-shaped tracks in the mud. Although the night was clear, there was no moon. Charlie could hear Jukes cursing behind him. It was the first time Charlie had seen stars since coming to New York.

Tateo stopped at a chain link fence that stretched off to the right and left across the path. Jukes pushed Charlie up against it.

"This is close enough," he said. "Come, Tateo. Please."

Ignoring him, Tateo turned right along the fence. The ground was soft and overgrown with reeds. Jukes grabbed Charlie's arm and pushed him after Tateo.

"You better be fucking grateful," said Jukes, "that's all I can say."

Charlie's feet were wet and he was cold. His bruises ached. He was even aware that he was hungry. But all these were distant feelings that required conscious notice, otherwise he was hardly aware of them. Mostly he was aware of Jukes' pistol. Secondly, he was aware of Tateo's small flashlight that snaked a trail through the reeds. Thirdly, there was the imminence of his own death. He could hardly believe that, despite his fear. Beyond those feelings, Charlie was aware of a kind of indignation that Tateo and Jukes thought they could get rid of him so simply. He wanted to hurt them and felt frustrated by his powerlessness. Ever since leaving Manhattan, he had been straining against the necktie that bound his hands, but, although he had loosened it, he still couldn't pull his hands free.

Tateo had stopped and Charlie almost bumped up against him. He flashed his light on a hole in the fence. "I'll go through first."

Beyond the fence was a pile of steel drums, lying on their sides and lined up in a row, layer upon layer. The three men climbed through the hole. Tateo led the way around to the left of the drums, then paused at the edge of a small field littered with rusting containers, lids, pieces of wood and cardboard, rubber tires. Thirty feet away was another pile of drums, perhaps eight layers high and forty feet long. Several hundred yards beyond it was a large corrugated metal warehouse lit by half a dozen yellow arc lights. A row of semitrailers was lined up to the left of the warehouse. There were also more piles of steel drums, some rusted, some new and painted black. A junked Corvair was lying on its roof near a pile of lumber, wooden crates, sheets of plywood scattered like large playing cards.

"Pretty isn't it," said Jukes. "This is where I'm coming on my honeymoon."

Quietly, Tateo began to cross the small field toward the nearest pile of drums. Jukes gave Charlie a shove. They had to keep walking around rusting containers and avoid tripping on lids, old two-by-fours, tires. The ground was covered with cinders. Charlie glanced around him. If he could break away, then he might stand a chance in this maze of barrels, semitrailers, junked cars and general desolation. Looking back at Jukes, he saw the top of the Empire State Building with its red light off in the distance. It was almost comforting.

Tateo had reached the pile of steel drums and appeared to be counting. In his left hand, he held an iron bar and used it to point at the drums.

"That's it. The tenth one."

"We'll put you in adjoining barrels," whispered Jukes. "Just like the fuckin' Ritz."

While Jukes held the flashlight, Tateo pried the lid off the drum with the iron bar. With his other hand, Jukes kept his pistol pointed at Charlie who stood slightly to their left, about fifteen feet from the end of the row.

The lid came off all of a sudden, clattering to the ground.

163

Tateo stumbled back. The smell of decomposing flesh seemed to surge out of the barrel. It was like a hand slapped over their noses. Very slowly, as the light shown on the open drum, a head and shoulders toppled back onto the ground.

"Smells like 'Nam," said Jukes. "There's Sammy. Take a look at him." He shone the light on the dead man's face.

Charlie was reminded of moldy bread. The face was grey and puffy, as if the person had been holding his breath day after day, waiting for this moment. A watchdog began to bark by the warehouse. As he looked at the blond hair, the empty blue eyes staring up at the sky, Charlie felt sadder than he would have believed possible. He thought of the man he had talked to in California.

"That's not Sam Cheney," he said. "It's Peter Bonenfant, his roommate."

29

THE BARKING grew louder. Charlie knew that after this moment he would have no further chances. As Jukes and Tateo stared down at the body, he stepped forward and kicked Jukes' knee, knocking him off balance. Jukes swore and stumbled against Tateo. Aiming high, Charlie kicked him again, trying for his groin. Jukes fell back, dropping the flashlight and grabbing at Tateo. Both men were stumbling, attempting to keep themselves from falling onto the body of Peter Bonenfant. Charlie turned and ran.

As he reached the end of the row of barrels, he saw some blurred movement to his left. Tateo shouted, "The dog! Get the dog!"

There was a shot and a yelp, then a second shot. Charlie didn't pause; bent over, scurrying more than running, he crossed a small, open yard toward another pile of barrels. Several spotlights went on near the warehouse, lighting up the whole area. Charlie twisted and turned to avoid tripping over the pieces of metal and wood littering the ground.

Reaching the barrels, he ducked behind them, looking for a temporary hiding place. He saw a small tarpaper shack about ten yards to his right. Scattered around it were square bales of paper or cardboard. Crouching down, he ran for the shed.

They were rags. Charlie squeezed himself between a damp, smelly bundle and the corner of the shed. The tarpaper was rough and studded with nails. Hoping to cut Driscoll's necktie, Charlie began to rub it against the building. He kept looking to his left but it was darker on this side of the barrels and he could see nothing, nor hear any sound.

The tie broke. Charlie stayed where he was, rubbing his wrists. There was still no sign of Tateo and Jukes. Ten yards in front of him the row of barrels rose up like a high wall about forty feet long. Above the barrels was the glow of the lights. Charlie began to look for a weapon. He felt around on the ground, picking up and discarding about a dozen rocks before settling on two that were the comfortable size of baseballs.

He felt exhilarated, as if his body were stronger, his senses keener. Although afraid, he felt himself capable of outwitting his enemies. It didn't occur to him that he was submitting to a new fantasy. Already he was searching for the words with which to describe his adventure to his friends in Saratoga.

He knew, consciously knew, that he was in danger of being killed, but that fact was too large for his imagination. Unable to conceive of a world in which he didn't exist, his ignorance saved him from panic, while the element of game allowed him to act calmly, even bravely. He crept about ten feet to the bale of rags nearest the containers.

There was a noise of metal against metal, and Charlie's bravery disappeared. Looking to his left, he saw someone standing at the end of the row of barrels about thirty feet away. It was hardly a person at all, just a black shape against the darkness. It began to move forward, very slowly, as if waiting for the slightest sound. Charlie couldn't tell if it was Tateo or Jukes, but his fear made him think

166

of Tateo. He wanted to run, but forced himself to stay motionless. As the figure came closer, Charlie could hear the crunch of cinders.

He didn't trust himself not to betray his position. The sound of his pulse, his heart and breathing—he was certain these would give him away. The figure had stopped and appeared to be listening.

Balancing one of the rocks in his hand, Charlie drew back his arm and hurled the rock over the pile of barrels. There was a clang as it hit some metal object in the further yard. The figure remained motionless, then, as Charlie began to think he had been found out, it turned silently and hurried back the way it had come.

When Charlie was sure it was gone, he crept back to the tarpaper shed. Beyond the shed was a field littered with broken barrels and lids. In the center of the field was a burned-out car. Charlie made his way toward it. He had emerged from his fantasy and wanted to get away as fast as possible.

The car was little more than a rusted shell. The wheels were gone and its trunk and hood were missing. Charlie crouched down behind it, watching the end of the barrels where the figure had disappeared. From his new position, he could also see the warehouse, the lawn in front of it and a driveway leading to a high gate. There were lights in several windows, and a pickup truck was parked by the side entrance.

As he began to relax and feel less frightened, Charlie became aware of the cold and the pains in his body. They were not small, located pains, but whole areas; and Charlie imagined black and blue marks like continents against the white of his skin. He knew he had to get away, but he was afraid of going back to the hole in the fence. His only consolation was that Tateo and Jukes must also be afraid;

167

not of him but of the watchman or police.

Looking behind him, Charlie could just make out the chain link fence and see where it turned left toward the gate. Near the gate was a small flood-lit sign: *Freeman Container Company*, surrounded by low shrubbery. Beyond the gate was a road, and on the other side of it was another warehouse and a line of semitrailers.

Not wishing to go directly to the gate, Charlie crouched down and ran toward the fence twenty feet behind him. He hoped to find another hole. As he moved along, he kept thinking he saw Tateo creeping up behind him. The thought brought him near panic and he forced himself to empty his mind.

The fence was eight feet high and topped with barbed wire. There were no holes and no way he could crawl under. Charlie told himself that if it weren't for his cracked ribs, he might be able to climb over at the corner or at the gate where there were support posts, but he knew that was a lie. Even as a young man in the army, he would not have been able to climb the fence.

He had expected the gate to be locked before he reached it, so that was only a minor disappointment, but he was surprised by the loneliness of being on the wrong side of a locked gate. Deciding that to climb was his only hope, Charlie had just begun to look for a handhold when he saw headlights coming down the road. He turned and ran back to the sign, *Freeman Container Company*, and lay down between it and the shrubbery.

A police car drew up to the fence. After a moment, a man hurried out of the warehouse and unlocked the gate. The police car drove through it slowly with its lights off. Charlie could hear the watchman talking but he couldn't make out the words. He was almost as afraid of being caught by the police as being found by Tateo.

Lying under the bushes, Charlie saw the watchman climb into the back seat of the police car. After a few seconds, the car drove slowly around the side of the warehouse. Almost before it was out of sight, Charlie was up and running for the gate. He passed through it and turned down the road. His exhilaration returned. He wanted to tell someone about his adventure. He hurried down the center of the road, half running, half jogging.

He thought of the time that Butch Cassidy kept Kid Curry from shooting Woodcock, the express car guard on the Union Pacific's Overland Flyer. Woodcock had refused to open the car door and had to be blasted out with dynamite. The explosion had stunned him. When Kid Curry rode forward to finish him off, Butch Cassidy stood in his way and said, "Leave him be, Kid. A man with nerve deserves not to be shot."

Jogging along the dark road somewhere in Secaucus, Charlie repeated to himself, "A man with nerve deserves not to be shot."

30

IT WAS PAST ONE when Charlie got back to Manhattan. After walking for several miles, he had been picked up by four teenagers in a dark purple 1949 Mercury. It was the kind of car that Charlie had once coveted, with tinted blue glass and a roof which had been lowered so the windshield was no more than a foot high. The seats were covered with blond tuck-and-roll upholstery.

Drunk and jovial, the kids had driven him directly to Victor's apartment, refusing to take any money except for gas and tolls. A frizzy-haired girl in the back seat had told him he looked like her father. Given his present condition, Charlie felt sorry for her.

Victor came up and let him in. "I hope you had a good time making yourself look like that."

"If anyone asks, just say you haven't seen me."

"Mister, the way you look, I wouldn't want to admit it."

Victor led the way back to his apartment. He had on a dark green robe of some shiny material with wide, black lapels. The cord at his waist was tipped with yellow tassels. Charlie saw there were blankets and sheets on the couch.

Going into the kitchen, Victor said, "I didn't know if you'd come back, but I figured if you did then you'd want a place to sleep."

170

He reappeared with the bottle of Jack Daniels and two glasses. The cat jumped from the couch, made a small leap for the yellow tassels, missed and began washing itself.

"Moshe's been sleeping on the blankets but I didn't figure you'd mind." Victor handed Charlie a glass half full of whiskey. "Bet you're surprised to see any of this stuff left. Well, I'd of finished it if it weren't for the cops."

"Cops?" Charlie had sat down on the couch and was—as his mother used to say—resting his eyes.

"That's right." Victor filled his glass three quarters full, then went back to the brown chair. Moshe made another unsuccessful snatch for the yellow tassels. Victor didn't seem to notice.

"What about the cops?" asked Charlie.

Victor shook his head. "I'm not supposed to have anything to do with you."

Charlie sipped his whiskey and waited. He thought again of kicking Jukes' knee and hiding by the tarpaper shed.

"Why didn't you say you'd been talking to the cops?" asked Victor after a minute. "At least you might of warned me."

"What happened?"

"They came bombing in here with a search warrant. Wanted to see Sam Cheney's apartment. So I let 'em in and they poked around."

"Who was it?"

"Cops, that's all."

Charlie rubbed his chin with his fist. He needed a shave and wished he could spend several hours in a bathtub. "Someone must have been in charge."

"Yeah, a big guy. Name like a sneeze."

"Zack."

Victor nodded. "He asked me all kinds of questions about Sam Cheney and Peter Bonenfant. What the fuck could I tell him? Then he asked if I knew you and if I'd let anyone into Cheney's apartment. I said you'd been around but was I going to break the law? Not on your ass. Good thing I put your suitcase in the closet."

Charlie guessed that Peter Bonenfant's father had called the police. "Did he believe you?"

"Sure, why not? He's still going to nail me, though. Those cops showed up around eight. Then an hour later a whole new set showed up with cameras and stuff like that, and they were dusting for fingerprints just like I seen 'em do on TV. I don't suppose you wore gloves this afternoon."

Despite Victor's nonchalance, Charlie knew he was upset, and he felt guilty for jeopardizing his job. "Maybe they won't know the prints are mine."

Victor rolled his eyes. "Sure. We'll cut off your fingers and feed 'em to the fish, and when the cops come back to take your prints we'll say, 'Tough luck, copper, I'm outta prints right now.' Believe-you-me, I lose my job over this and I'm coming up to Saratoga and you can talk to those rich friends of yours and find me another. I'm not particular what it is."

Charlie couldn't tell if Victor was serious. "I don't have any rich friends in Saratoga."

"Don't give me that, you were even talking about them. Vanderbilts, Whitneys, Markeys, Phipps. I read the papers; I know their names. Just give them a call."

"To tell the truth," said Charlie, "I wouldn't know a Vanderbilt if he came up and punched me in the eye."

Victor seemed indignant. He put his glass on the floor as if he couldn't drink and argue at the same time. "You live right there with 'em. What the hell you been doing all your life?"

"That's not how it works," said Charlie patiently, "I know their summer houses and we get told when they come into town. I may even recognize their cars or know how much some Whitney paid for a horse at the auction. I even went to the auction once, coupla years ago. They sell more'n sixty yearlings a day for four days, make over $8 million. You see these guys buying a $100,000 horse by raising a little finger. You can't get inside without a ticket and you can't get a ticket unless your credit's good. Me and a crowd of other people looked in through the big windows. One cheap horse, it was $7,000. I told myself I could afford that. Mortgage my house, sell my car. I'd have my own race horse, except that for $7,000 it's bound to be a loser, and training and upkeep costs about $20 a day. So there I'd be with an untrained horse in my garage which the bank wants to repossess. Maybe I could take the horse out on Sundays, you know, walk it around the block, because I couldn't ride it. Their legs are too spindly or something. Maybe I could let little kids ride it. Anyway at this auction there was a bar and I went to the bar. I mean, I can't buy a horse but I can still afford Molsons. Money, jewels, you're almost blinded. I found myself thinking like a communist or something. I didn't go back."

Victor leaned forward and put his elbows on his knees. "So if I get fired, you can't get me a new job."

"Maybe I could. Did you know that Wyatt Earp only got paid $2.50 a month for being marshal of Dodge City?"

"What's that got to do with anything?"

Charlie stood up. "Not much. It makes me happy. Where's my bag? I've got to change my clothes and go out again. And can you let me have a key so I can get back in?"

Victor waved his arm behind him. "Your bag's in the closet. If I'd known you were going to be this much trouble, I'd never of let you in. Baby face or no baby face."

Charlie's pants were torn and so were the pair he had worn

the previous night. The light grey pair he had worn down on Monday were simply dirty. He put them on along with a soiled white shirt.

Victor poured himself some more whiskey. He was grinning and appeared to take pleasure in Charlie's discomforts. "Way you're going you should of brought down a Saratoga trunk. You think Sam Cheney's dead?"

In his mind, Charlie again saw the lid fall off the metal drum, and the head and shoulders of Peter Bonenfant flop back to the ground. He could almost smell the stench. "No, he's probably as healthy as you are. Can I borrow a jacket?"

"Help yourself. Where you going this time of night?"

Charlie put on a blue, waist-length, wool jacket. He thought it looked a little like the kind baseball managers wore. That made him feel better even though the jacket was several sizes too large. "I'm going over to see Sam's girlfriend."

Victor tossed him a key and Charlie caught it. "Business or pleasure?"

Charlie fastened the snaps on the jacket. "You're a rude son-of-a-bitch, you know that?"

"Everyone needs a hobby."

31

ASSUMING that Stacy was still watched by the police, Charlie took a cab to her building. It was 2:30 by the time he got there. The driver didn't want to wait. Charlie gave him $10 and one of the cards identifying him as a Saratoga Springs police sergeant.

"That's okay, buddy, my brother-in-law he gave me some cards for Christmas, said I was the Queen of Sheba."

Inside the foyer, Charlie pressed the purple button for Stacy's apartment, and kept pressing it for nearly a minute. There was a crackling noise as Stacy's voice came through the small speaker.

"Who is it?"

"Charlie. I want to talk."

"We have nothing to talk about."

"If you don't let me in, I'll go to the police."

There was a pause. Charlie made star-shaped patterns with his thumb print on the polished brass.

"What for?" asked Stacy.

"I'll tell them where to find Peter Bonenfant's body." Charlie was fairly certain that Tateo and Jukes had moved the body, but he doubted they had taken it far.

"I'm coming down."

Charlie waited. Apart from his cab, the street seemed

empty. Zack probably had a man in one of the surrounding buildings. Charlie imagined him picking up the phone.

Stacy appeared at the door in jeans, a blue sweater and brown terrycloth slippers. Charlie found himself staring at her thin face, looking for the lines that would turn into wrinkles then creases as she got older. Her black hair hung loosely down her back.

"Let's go upstairs," she said.

They stood in the lobby by the bank of mailboxes. "We can talk here."

"It's more private upstairs."

They took the elevator and waited for it to arrive at the third floor like two strangers, even though the elevator was the size of a large bathtub. Charlie didn't want to go into her apartment and suspected a trap. He knew, however, that given his present state of mind, he would suspect a trap in a Salvation Army meeting hall.

He wasn't comfortable until he had looked in her closet, bathroom and kitchenette. Then he stayed by the front door. He had begun to feel foolish in Victor's dark blue jacket, feeling that Baseball Coach was not the image he cared to project.

"Do you want to look under the bed?" asked Stacy. She had sat down on the blue couch and looked bored.

Charlie stayed where he was. "When I got beat up last night," he said, "you led me right into it. You knew Sam was out there waiting with some other guy. At first I thought it was Peter Bonenfant, but he's dead. Even when it happened, I knew you'd set me up, but I was such a fool I wouldn't let myself believe it."

The combination of a high ceiling and not much furniture made Charlie's voice echo against the bare white walls. Stacy sat in the middle of the couch with her legs curled up under her.

"Did Sam tell you to seduce me as well?" Charlie asked. "All that junk about numbers. You must have really thought I was an idiot when I told you my name was Chuck. . . ."

It depressed him that he couldn't speak to her coldly, that he wanted to ask her to run away with him to the Yukon where they would build a log cabin and live on bear meat and salmon. He told himself that it was the idea of a young woman he loved, not Stacy. He had fallen victim to her interest and flattery. Charlie tried to work up some anger, but continued to feel sad. He carefully stayed by the door.

"I know about the cocaine and where it's coming from," he said. "I know that Sam used Bonenfant to bring money from California and as a decoy. I know the names of the guys that killed him and will kill Sam if they get the chance. I know that Sam plans to pick up the cocaine to-morrow."

"So? Go to the police."

Charlie shook his head. "I came down here to find Sam and that's what I mean to do. I've been bothering about him for his whole life, a stupid sort of bothering that hasn't led anywhere. Now I'm done with it. He wants to get himself killed or thrown in jail, that's his business. But I want to see him, just talk to him, person to person."

Stacy hadn't moved. "You think he's your son, don't you."

"No. His mother used to tell me that Sam was my son, but she was lying. I don't have any children."

"I don't know where Sam is."

Charlie looked at her sadly. "Yes you do. You're going to set up a meeting for early this morning. I'll call you at seven. If you refuse or if he refuses to see me, I'll go to the police. If he does see me and tries any funny stuff, I'll

177

make sure the police still find out about it. All I want is to talk to him. It'll take five minutes, then I'll go back to Saratoga."

Stacy was silent for a while. In her jeans and blue sweater, she looked like part of the blue couch: something soft and comfortable. She seemed to be looking at a blank spot on the wall.

"I'll call him," she said at last.

"Good."

"What are you going to do now?"

"Go back and get a few hours' sleep."

"Do you want to stay here?"

"I've got a cab outside."

"Send it away."

Charlie was startled by the amount of desire she could cause in him. It made him feel like his body's puppet. He told himself that nothing that had happened made any difference. He could sleep with her, spend the night with her, and it would be a gift: a free period in which there would be no fault or responsibility. Tomorrow he would go back to Saratoga, get some job as a Pinkerton guard and pursue his next forty-one years. He argued that she was something he owed himself. They would have one night without any words.

"I'd like to stay," said Charlie, "but I don't know who you are. Goodnight, Stacy. I'll call you at seven. I'm sorry things didn't work out."

178

32

CHARLIE HAD THE CAB drop him off at Cooper Union, then walked the last three blocks. Not only would Zack learn of his visit to Stacy's, he would learn the number of his cab as well. There was no point in leading him to Victor.

As Charlie unlocked the door, he heard Victor snoring. It was a mellow rumble like the '49 Mercury which had brought him back to Manhattan. Were there customized Mercs in the Yukon? Charlie saw a note on the couch and went to pick it up.

"There's Heinekens and sliced ham in the fridge. Make yourself at home. Sorry I finished the Jack Daniels. Vic."

Charlie made himself a ham and cheese sandwich, then came back and ate it on the couch. He hadn't noticed the ham earlier and suspected Victor had bought it with him in mind. The light was off in the aquarium. As he ate, Charlie considered the sleeping habits of fish to keep from thinking about Stacy. It was a partial success. Moshe slept on the pillow beside him. Despite his allergy, Charlie was comforted by the cat's presence.

Although tired, he knew he wouldn't sleep. He kept thinking of Saratoga and the people who would call him a fool for staying in New York. He could imagine the boredom he would feel when listening to them, and then felt bored with himself for worrying about what other people thought. There were more important losses to consider.

Along with the loss of his job, Charlie would have to resign from The Protective and Benevolent Association. That meant quitting as assistant coach of the Pony League team which the association sponsored. He regretted that. He remembered that his eldest cousin's construction company sponsored a team in the Babe Ruth League. Maybe they could use him. It seemed a pity that his trip to New York had coincided with the beginning of baseball season.

Not that Charlie had ever been much of a player. In school he had never made the team despite the hours he had practiced fielding fake flies from the roof of his uncle's two-story house. During his senior year, he had been promoted equipment manager.

But neither was he a terrible player. Of the twenty kids that used to meet on Saturdays at the diamond across from St. Clements, Charlie would be picked about sixth by the captains choosing up sides. A reliable right fielder, he would wait patiently all afternoon, grabbing a few bouncing grounders while the aggressive center fielder shagged the pop flies. At bat he could be counted on for a base hit, depending on the skill of the opposing shortstop.

Charlie went out to the kitchen for another beer. As he moved, he was again aware of the pains in his body. He had not been surprised that Sam had beaten him up. Sam was a person of few loyalties, and Charlie had never pretended to believe that Sam was grateful for any of the help he had given him. Indeed, it was this outlaw quality, this chosen isolation, that Charlie almost admired.

Charlie returned to the couch, pausing only to look at the fish. They didn't seem asleep. Despite his regret at losing his job and the respect of his acquaintances, Charlie

180

knew that part of him felt pleased. He too, if only for a short time, had chosen isolation, had shared this outlaw quality. He had overthrown his established life. The fact that he would return to Saratoga to begin some new but completely similar life didn't matter. It was the overthrow that was important.

He might find a job with the sheriff's department or become a guard at the county jail or join the police force of some small town. That didn't matter. He even amused himself with the idea of becoming a guard at the National Museum of Racing. It seemed fitting that the son of a man dedicated to betting on losers should spend his life protecting the mementoes of the horses that had won: the saddle used by Johnny Loftus when he rode Man o' War, the cane given to Tod Sloan by King Edward VII.

Charlie also felt pleased at the way he had handled himself. Never before had he been in a situation where his life was in such danger, and although he had experienced five hours of extreme fear, he had done nothing to be ashamed of. In his fantasies, he might see himself as capturing Tateo and Jukes single-handed, but that would have been impossible without a gun and improbable with one. It had been enough to escape, while the memory of that escape would be a source of pleasure for a long time.

Already he felt pride. In his years as a policeman, he had rarely felt afraid. Not much had happened. There had been men who resisted arrest, mostly drunks, with whom he might briefly struggle. Once a sixteen-year-old boy had threatened him with a gun when Charlie had come to arrest him for robbing a gas station. Once a woman had attacked him with a knife during a family trouble run. The fear in those instances had come afterward when he began to imagine what might have happened.

His inexperience with fear always led Charlie to wonder

how he would handle himself, and worry that he might not behave with dignity. In his reading of criminal history, Charlie would pay particular attention to how some outlaw met his death, and admire his bravery while deploring his crime. When Charlie felt generally overwhelmed by the world, he would recall these examples and feel consoled. For instance, there was Francis "Two-Gun" Crowley who sauntered up to the electric chair in Sing Sing smoking a cigar. As the straps were adjusted, he flicked the cigar at the reporters, and hit one in the forehead. "Give my love to mother," he said. Then the current was turned on.

Against this, Charlie would remember the story of a man he had once met in Saratoga whose squad of fifteen men had been captured by the Germans at the end of the war. The Germans were retreating and had no time for prisoners. They had started to machine gun them, and killed eight soldiers before stopped by their captain. As he waited to be shot, Charlie's acquaintance had lost control of his bowels and fouled himself.

"Walked ten miles with shit in my pants. Fuckin' krauts knew what I'd done. Laugh, they thought it was a fuckin' joke."

Charlie had always been afraid he might do that. But now, although he might lose his job and be criticized by people in Saratoga, he could recall his escape from Tateo and Jukes and know he had behaved with dignity. Foolishly perhaps, but with dignity.

FRIDAY

33

CHARLIE AND STACY walked along the north side
of Fulton Street toward the Fulton Fish Market and Pier 16
where they would meet Sam Cheney. Charlie carried his
canvas suitcase. It was 8:45 and the morning was bright,
blue and chilly enough to make Charlie regret that he had
turned down Victor's offer of a sweater. He was freezing in
his grey sport coat.

Charlie had said good-bye to Victor at 7:30. Victor promised to visit, maybe right away if he lost his job, or in
August during the races when he could search out a real
Vanderbilt or Whitney. Charlie promised to get back down
to New York. Both men knew they probably wouldn't see
each other again.

When he had called Stacy, she told him to be in front of
St. Paul's Chapel on Broadway at Fulton Street at 8:30.
He found her dressed in jeans and a brown quilted jacket.
She wore dark glasses and her hair was hidden by a brown
and white scarf.

Seeing her, Charlie was grateful that she had obscured
her face. She could have been almost anybody. As he
thought that, he realized his feelings for Gladys had been
transferred to Stacy, as if he had scraped together a remembered emotion, revitalized it and presented it to Stacy as

something new and original.

This morning, however, she wanted none of it. She was cool, businesslike and, after nodding to him, had turned down Fulton Street expecting him to follow. Charlie looked regretfully at her back. He had never been in this part of the city before and at least would have liked a moment to glance in at the Chapel and its small graveyard. There was no telling who might be buried there.

The sidewalks and streets were crowded with people hurrying to work, rush hour traffic, produce and delivery trucks. Charlie had to walk quickly to keep up with Stacy. Off to his right he saw the beginnings of the financial district and the sixty-five-story Chase Manhattan Bank Building, although he didn't realize that was what it was.

Charlie kept asking himself what he would say to Sam Cheney. It was almost as if there were two of them: the one in Charlie's imagination and the flesh and blood Sam Cheney who he would see that morning. Charlie knew that although the real Sam might beat him up, it was the imaginary one that did the most damage. Hadn't he brought him to New York? By meeting him, Charlie hoped the two Sams would be brought together.

They crossed Water Street and entered the area known as South Street Seaport Museum. A row of four-story Federal-style buildings with red paint flaking off their bricks stretched off to the right. There were several small fish markets, restaurants, a book and chart store and a store selling marine supplies and foul weather gear. Charlie sniffed the smell of fish. They had left the rush hour crowd at Water Street and here the sidewalks were almost empty. Stacy remained a few feet ahead of him. He called after her.

"Stacy, if you don't leave New York, you'll probably go to jail."

She kept walking, gave no sign of hearing what he had

186

said. Charlie thought even her back was beautiful.

"Sam's in a lot of trouble," he continued. "The best thing you can do is stay out of it."

She neither turned nor slowed down. Charlie started to say that he was warning her for her own good, then he stopped himself, afraid that he was only protecting his conscience from whatever might happen. He disliked being jealous of Sam Cheney.

They stopped at South Street to wait for a gap in the traffic. Above them rose the elevated East River drive. After a minute, they made a dash to the other side. The cars honked but didn't slow down. A small bald man in a red Pinto gave Charlie the finger. Closer to the market the smell of fish was much stronger.

They threaded their way between about thirty parked cars to the gate of Pier 16. As they passed through the gate, Charlie noticed a young man standing off to his right by a small information booth. He was about twenty-three and wore jeans, a brown leather jacket and cowboy boots. The man looked at Charlie, then looked away.

Charlie touched Stacy's shoulder. "Is that Sam's buddy over there? He's the other guy that beat me up, right?"

Stacy ignored him and continued quickly along the pier. To their left was a grey, one-story, pre-fab restaurant. Orange life preservers hung in its windows. Moored to the pier beyond the restaurant were a number of old ships. To their right was the *Wavertree*, a huge, iron-hulled, square-rigged cargo ship. Beyond it was a red water tender that looked like a tug boat. Rows of blue metal chairs were lined up around the restaurant and along the edge of the pier. On the far side of the pier was moored a large ferry boat, *The Robert Fulton*, painted white with red trim. Beyond it, at the end of the pier, was the lightship *Ambrose*. Charlie looked ahead at the East River and the massive sweep of the Brooklyn Bridge against the blue sky. There was no one else in sight.

Stacy led the way toward the lightship. The bright red of its hull was interrupted only by the white letters of its name: *Ambrose*. The rest of the ship was white except for the two masts and funnel which were yellowish brown. Charlie thought the ship was about 100 feet long.

Stacy went up the gangplank at the stern of the ship. As Charlie followed her, he saw a young man in a brown corduroy jacket leaning over the rail. Across the river was Brooklyn, and directly across were docks and a large yellow building with the word *Watchtower* on its roof in red letters. Above the letters was a lighted sign indicating that the time was 8:58 and the temperature 39 degrees.

The man at the rail was thin with long, black, curly hair that fell past his neck and came to a point like the point of a shovel. He had on light brown corduroy pants and black tennis shoes. Although he must have heard their footsteps, he didn't move until Charlie said his name: "Sam Cheney."

Sam turned. Without seeing his face, it had been possible to give him all sorts of qualities, but looking at him now Charlie thought he saw proof of the faults he had hoped to find. The narrow chin, the brown eyes slanted like his mother's, the thinness of his face, even his pallor: these for Charlie became evidence of Sam's greed and small-mindedness, a smug and undeserved self-confidence. He had full lips and a mouth too small for his teeth. Under his jacket, he wore a white Indian shirt and a turquoise and silver necklace. Charlie had come intending to dislike Sam, and from his appearance he drew the reasons for his dislike. It became his strongest criticism of Stacy that she could prefer such a person.

For nearly half a minute, Sam stared at Charlie without speaking. Charlie knew he was meant to feel intimidated. He smiled slightly.

188

"You know, you've killed me," said Sam. "You couldn't of killed me any better if you'd shot me yourself." He spoke softly.

Charlie shook his head. It was colder on the river and he crossed his arms, tucking his hands under his elbows.

"Those two guys, they won't leave town until I'm dead. What the fuck you come down here for anyway? It was none of your business."

Charlie began to say that Gladys had been worried. It sounded silly. He wondered if it were even true. "You're responsible for whatever's happened, Sam." He winced at the paternal tone. It was unfortunate that Sam was such a difficult young man to love. If Sam had ever responded to his fatherly affection, Charlie would have done anything for him.

Sam grew angrier. "My whole fucking life you been butting in, and just when I think I'm free of you, shit, here you come again. What'd you tell those guys anyway?"

"They know they killed Peter Bonenfant."

"And the cops, what do they know?"

While Charlie had no wish to help Zack, neither did he wish to interfere. "They're expecting you to meet a man at The Lamplighter later today."

Sam appeared relieved. In his anger, however, he looked like a possum or weasel cornered by terriers. It made his crowded teeth seem pointier.

"That's something at least," he said. "Jesus, I can't believe how you've fucked things up. I'll bet you'll be really happy when those guys kill me."

Charlie didn't want to talk anymore. Having seen Sam and spoken to him, he wanted to leave. He thought himself freed of the illusions he had once had, and to stay any longer would only stress the mistakes he had made about Sam during the past fifteen years. Seeing him, he was free of him. He would return to Saratoga.

"Where's my wallet?" he asked.

"What d'you mean?"

"My wallet, you stole it the other night when you beat me up, you and that guy at the end of the pier."

"I don't know what you're talking about."

Charlie looked away at the blue sky, the Brooklyn Bridge, the river leading out to the ocean beyond. It seemed too nice a day for this. He was aware of Stacy standing behind him to his left. He imagined a submarine carrying them off to some far place.

"Early last month," Charlie began, "you learned you could buy some cocaine cheap. You learned it from a guy in Los Angeles who supplies you with marijuana that you sell here in New York. You started getting some money together and called your friend Peter Bonenfant in San Diego, telling him you had a job for him at the clothing store where you worked. That was a lie. You had no job, but you wanted him here in case there was trouble from the real owners of the cocaine, and you wanted him to pick up an envelope of money from your partner in Los Angeles. Peter Bonenfant was looking forward to coming to New York. What was he here, nine days, before he got killed?

"You could have prevented that. Your mother talked to Bonenfant on Saturday, March 22. That's the day he was murdered. He was worried about you, said you hadn't been home all night. What I think is that you heard these guys were looking for you so you hid, leaving Bonenfant in your apartment. You didn't even warn him. Maybe they had seen him in California, and maybe that's why you had him pick up the money. In any case, he never had a chance. They came to your apartment and killed him, thinking he was you. Nice friend you are.

"When I arrived, you were afraid I'd mess up your cocaine deal. You got Stacy to pump me for information and when I didn't leave you and a buddy beat me up and took my wallet and gun. Did you tell Stacy to fuck me too?"

As Charlie said that, Sam lunged at him. Charlie stepped aside. What had worked once would work again. Charlie kicked Sam in the left knee. Sam yelled, fell back against the railing, then dropped to the deck. Charlie glanced guiltily at Stacy, but she stood against the cabin watching Sam as if he were an experiment.

Turning back toward Sam, Charlie saw him reach for something under his jacket. He guessed what it was. He moved forward and when Sam drew a revolver, Charlie kicked his wrist, sending the gun in a high arc over the railing and into the East River. It was only when he saw the splash that Charlie realized it was his own revolver. He raised his foot again.

"Don't hurt me!" Sam tried to shield his head with his arm. Charlie knew that if he kicked him once, he wouldn't be able to stop. He stepped back.

"Where's my wallet?"

"I don't know. I took the money, then dumped it. Tossed it into a trash can."

"You owe me thirty bucks, give it to me."

"I don't have it."

"Give it to me before I kick you to pieces."

Sam got to his feet, holding his wrist where Charlie had kicked it. He took out his wallet and gave Charlie $30. Charlie was tempted to throw the wallet into the river but decided that was too petty. He didn't really care about the $30, but he wanted something. His badge had been in his wallet, and Sam had taken it more easily than Chief Peterson could have done. For a moment it seemed he had traded his badge for his business cards only because of Stacy's flattery: *Charles F. Bradshaw, Sergeant.*

Sam leaned against the railing, trying to rub his wrist and knee at the same time. Charlie wanted to take Stacy's arm and say, "Can't you see how cheap he is? How could you have betrayed me for someone like that?" It was hard to stop thinking about it.

"Are you going to the police?" said Sam.

"I told you I wasn't."

"What're you going to do?"

"Go back to Saratoga."

"You going to see my mother?"

"Not if I can help it. I just wanted to find you, that's all."

"Thanks a fuckin' lot."

Charlie began to turn away, then stopped. "Sam, you might just forget about the cocaine. Leave the city. The police were in your apartment last night and found bloodstains. They'll match it with Peter Bonenfant as soon as they have his blood type."

Sam shook his head. "It's too good a chance. Look, Charlie, you help me with the cops and I'll let you in on this. It could mean $5,000."

The only responses open to Charlie were physical and violent. Ignoring Sam, he turned toward Stacy. She had taken off her dark glasses and looked back at him with her green eyes. Her cheeks were pink from the cold. He wanted to touch her but was afraid to.

"If you come with me now," he told her, "you'll be all right."

"Is that a bribe?" There was no expression on her face.

"You just walk away with me now, and I'll give you money to get out of the city. I mean no more than that."

She lowered her head. "I'm staying with Sam."

"Because of those numbers? What's he done for you?"

Stacy reached out, touched Charlie's arm, then moved

back. "You're a nice man. I'm sorry you were hurt." Her face was still expressionless. She stuck her hands in the pockets of her brown coat and turned away toward the Brooklyn Bridge.

Without saying anything else, he walked away from her and down the gangplank of the Ambrose. When Charlie reached the pier, Sam called after him, "You sure you're not going to the cops?"

"You're a punk, Sam Cheney," said Charlie without looking back. As he left the pier, he saw the young man in boots still playing lookout by the information booth. Charlie called to him, "You're a punk too!"

34

CHARLIE AGAIN SAT across from Gate 27 in the lower concourse of Port Authority Bus Terminal. It was 10:15 and he was waiting for the eleven o'clock bus to Saratoga Springs. His green plaid canvas suitcase was wedged between his feet so he wouldn't forget it. Crowds of people streamed by in either direction. Charlie tried to calculate how many he could count in ten minutes. Certainly over a thousand. Upstairs a kindly information clerk had told him that nearly 7,500 buses used the terminal each day.

Charlie was attempting to avoid thinking about New York and Saratoga. It depressed him that his imagined quest so closely resembled a Shirley Temple movie. Had he really seen himself as rescuing little Sam Cheney and carrying him back to his mother? Nor could he say that the experience had made him any wiser. Next week, next year: he might again be tempted to submit himself to some story drawn from a 1930's film. It saddened him that he could set aside the rational portion of his mind and throw over the quiet routine of his life with such pleasure.

In any case it was over, or at least his part of it was over. Sam's pursuit of the cocaine, Tateo's pursuit of Sam, the machinery of the police—all that could work itself out

194

without him. Zack would win; he was strongest. Charlie had no desire to observe the details. To stay any longer would be the same as having been driven back to Saratoga earlier: it would mean submitting to the rules and definitions of other people.

Not that Charlie took any pleasure in going back to Saratoga. He dreaded having to deal with the problems he would find there. Already he had begun formulating answers to his wife's questions of why hadn't he called, where had he been, didn't he realize what he had lost or destroyed, didn't he care about her feelings. He thought of those times as a teenager when he had stayed out past his curfew, then stayed out even longer because he was afraid of the consequences of going home. Briefly, he asked himself if there weren't some other city where he could go.

Charlie did not regret any of his actions. He was excited by the memory of his bravery in New Jersey. He was pleased with the memory of Victor Plotz and his fish and Moshe the Enforcer. And although saddened by the memory of Stacy, it was something to know he was capable of such strong emotion.

He knew these memories would comfort him when he was back in Saratoga as Charlie Bradshaw: ex-youth officer, present stable guard, hardware-store salesman, museum guard, whatever. His cousins would find him a new job. He would take it. That might be weakness, but whenever he thought he was too weak, he would remember kicking Jukes in the knee.

It was now 10:30. Charlie would be boarding soon. He sat watching the stream of people. Perhaps it was like a movie where the crowd of 1,000 is actually 100 extras, each seen in ten different hats. As Charlie idly tried to penetrate the disguises of people he had seen before, he saw the two plainclothesmen.

Since they were walking directly toward him, they weren't difficult to spot. They were both six feet, between thirty-five and fifty and wore dark raincoats. They had the faces of men who might be foolish, but never silly.

Charlie considered running through Gate 27, leaping onto the bus and claiming sanctuary. But it was too late to do anything but look expectant.

"Charles Bradshaw?" They showed their badges.

Charlie nodded. He again thought of his business cards. They would probably think he was reaching for a weapon.

"You're to come with us."

"My bus is about to leave."

"We can't help that."

"Can't you tell Zack I've already left?"

"Want us to use cuffs?"

35

THE TWO PLAINCLOTHESMEN drove Charlie to a precinct station on 35th between Eighth and Ninth avenues. They neither spoke nor acknowledged his presence. The lobby of the precinct station was full of efficient-looking men, both in and out of uniform. No one looked at Charlie. He didn't suppose they were any different from Saratoga Springs policemen; but as he was led across the lobby to the stairs, he felt like a creature from another species, a smaller species.

Charlie was taken upstairs and led to an open doorway. Then, giving him a push, one of the plainclothesmen said, "Here he is," and left him.

Stumbling slightly, Charlie entered a large conference room with light blue walls and a map of the city of New York. Zack stood by a long table talking to three men who were sorting through a small pile of 8 x 10 photographs. He had on a brown suit, a tan shirt and a brown tie. His short grey hair was brushed up so it was perfectly flat on top. When he saw Charlie, he turned and began walking toward him. Charlie thought he looked like an angry bus conductor. He didn't feel like being yelled at. Zack stopped a foot away, close enough for Charlie to see a tiny patch of grey bristles under his nose which Zack had presumably missed while shaving.

The police lieutenant tapped Charlie on the chest with a thick index finger. "What'd you tell him?"

"Tell who?"

"Don't fuck with me. What'd you tell Sam Cheney?"

Charlie was angry with himself for feeling frightened. He told himself that he had finished his business in New York, and Zack could do nothing to interfere with it. Zack was six inches taller than he, and Charlie stared up at the pink roof of his mouth.

"I didn't tell him anything."

"Don't lie to me. What did you tell him?"

"Nothing."

Zack reached out and grabbed Charlie's grey jacket. "You little turd, you want to go to jail?"

Charlie didn't say anything. He didn't trust himself to speak calmly. What he wanted to do most was knee the policeman in the groin. At last he said, "Did you ever hear of Sam Bass?"

"Who?"

"He was a train robber and bank robber who got shot up in Round Tree, Texas, when one of his gang betrayed him to the Rangers. That was maybe in 1878."

Zack let him go. "Are you crazy?"

"Sam Bass was wounded but he managed to ride out of town. A little later Texas Ranger Major John B. Jones found him sitting on a farmer's front porch dying with a bullet in his stomach. Jones asked him what had happened to his gang. Sam Bass didn't answer. Jones asked him again and you know what Sam Bass said?"

Zack stood with his head tilted a little to the right. "What did he say, you crazy son-of-a-bitch?"

"He said, 'It's agin my trade to blow on my pals. If a man knows anything, he ought to die with it in him.' Then he said, 'The world is bobbing around.' Then he died."

Zack looked at Charlie, arms crossed, head still tilted to one side. Then he turned abruptly and took a few steps toward the table. He stopped and turned back. "You know, I heard you were dead. That's what the story was last night. You'd got yourself killed. You think I looked forward to calling Saratoga Springs and breaking the news? Lotta questions. Lotta bad publicity. Then one of my men saw you leaving that broad's building. You fuck her again? Jesus, you're just like a rabbit. You'd gotten yourself killed, this whole fuckin' thing would get blown up in the papers. I'd wind up in a precinct in Brooklyn. Brooklyn, shit. Mobile, Alabama. Why didn't you tell me about this Peter Bonenfant?"

Charlie shrugged and put down his suitcase. He looked at the map of New York City on the wall, trying to see where he had been. It made his legs ache. The three men at the table continued to sort through the photographs. They hadn't even glanced at Charlie. Maybe they thought he was delivering shirts. Charlie saw that the photographs were of Sam: Sam on the street, Sam in a park, Sam walking, running, standing still.

After a moment, he said, "I didn't owe you anything. I mean, I don't want to make it sound like you've hurt my feelings, but I don't owe you a darn thing. Why should I tell you about Peter Bonenfant?"

Zack stood with his hands in his back pockets. His body seemed made of square stones. There were no soft or rounded lines. "You're a prick."

"I take it you've talked to Bonenfant's father."

"Look, prick, I could have you put in jail. You'd never get out."

"And you talked to Driscoll. Did you arrest him?"

"It's too bad, prick, that you're not a cop in New York.

199

It'd give me pleasure to bust you. Bonenfant's dead, right?"

Charlie thought of saying that thanks to Zack he was no longer a cop anywhere. "He's been dead for nearly three weeks. I saw his body last night. It was crammed into a steel container someplace over in New Jersey. It's probably gone now."

"Tateo and Jukes?"

"That's right. Tateo's from New York. Apparently he used to drive a truck for this container place. The other guy, Jukes, he's from Los Angeles. Driscoll talked to you about them?"

Zack nodded. "Do me a favor and tell me what happened."

At first he didn't intend to, then he found himself talking about Driscoll and how he had been tricked, tied up and driven to New Jersey. About what had happened at the container company, Charlie only said, "When they looked at the body, I was able to get away. There was a watchdog and Jukes shot it. The watchman heard the noise. When the police came, I slipped out through the front gate." He was surprised at how simple it sounded.

Zack listened silently. With his jowls and square chin, he looked like a man in an advertisement for tires that Charlie used to see in *Colliers* and *The Saturday Evening Post*. When Charlie had finished, Zack went to use the telephone on the table near the three men.

The three men had stopped talking and were looking at their fingernails or the ceiling or the floor or their shoes or their watches. All three were in their mid-forties. They had short and neatly combed brown or grey hair. They wore dark suits. One wore glasses. Another had a small grey moustache. The third sucked on an empty pipe. Otherwise they could have had interchangeable parts. Charlie imagined they composed a Yugoslavian fact-finding team that had

200

been sent to New York for two weeks by the Yugoslavian government. Now they were waiting to be taken someplace and shown something. On the other hand, Charlie thought, perhaps I am being shown to them. He tried to imagine what they would say about him when they returned to Belgrade. He wondered what they were doing with the photographs of Sam.

Zack hung up the phone and walked back toward Charlie. "What did you tell Sam? Don't fuck with me now, it's important."

"I told him you were watching The Lamplighter. I said if he didn't leave town, he'd be arrested."

"Will he leave?"

"No. He's greedy and vain and he thinks he can outsmart you. He set Bonenfant up. It's Sam's fault he got killed."

For a second, Charlie saw the red lightship, the blue sky and the darker blue of the river, the Brooklyn Bridge with the Manhattan Bridge beyond it, Brooklyn itself like a city of mushrooms, the shipping yards, the blue river trailing out to a bluer sea, and Sam in his brown corduroy jacket leaning against the rail of the *Ambrose,* greedy, small-minded and spitting out words.

"I gave Sam a tremendous chance," continued Charlie, "Stacy too. I've done a lot of favors for Sam, but none as big as that one. How much does he figure to make?"

"He's buying for twenty; he could sell for at least sixty. I don't know what kind of deal he's got with his partner."

Charlie started to speak, call Sam names; he was sorry he hadn't kicked him again. Mostly he was sorry that he couldn't stop thinking about him. "What about Driscoll?" he asked.

"He's working for us now. Thinks it'll keep him out of jail."

"Will it?"

"Might."

"Can I get out of here now? I want to get back to Saratoga."

"We need you here for a bit. You're a witness. We'll have to get a statement. You know the routine. I want to keep an eye on you."

"What the hell for?" But Charlie already knew. It seemed unfair that he should be made to watch the details of Sam's arrest. He had finished his discoveries; there was nothing else he wanted to learn.

The phone rang before Zack could answer. While he waited, Charlie studied the map of New York. He noticed a park at the very bottom of the city: Battery Park. He imagined it full of pencils, pennies, lipstick containers, Kleenex, keys—objects that had fallen from the pockets of New Yorkers and rolled to the foot of the city. He was sorry he hadn't visited the park. He noticed it contained a statue of Verrazano, the Florentine merchant who had "found" Manhattan. Charlie seemed to remember that Verrazano had later found a tribe of cannibals in the Caribbean and they had eaten him.

36

"DOG WAS HIT TWICE. Once in the shoulder, once in the head. Not bad for quick shooting. Jersey police couldn't find Bonenfant's body, but there's a hole in the fence and a lotta footprints. Also tire tracks. It's a fucking swamp over there. They're dragging for the body. I wish 'em luck." Zack carefully reached in his shirt pocket and drew out a wrinkled Lucky Strike. Breaking it in two, he stuck one half in his mouth and put the other back in his pocket. "Trying to cut down," he told Charlie.

They were in an unmarked white Chevrolet driving south on West Street under the West Side Elevated Highway. Charlie didn't know their exact location, but several blocks back they had passed the entrance to the Holland Tunnel. The uneven paving stones made the car bounce like a worn-out carnival ride. Charlie was wedged in the front seat between Zack and the driver. In the back seat were three plainclothesmen looking exactly, Charlie thought, like See No Evil, Hear No Evil, Speak No Evil. It was 11:30. Occasionally Charlie caught a glimpse of the World Trade Center about a mile ahead of them.

"The way you were talking to Driscoll," Zack continued, "I knew he had to be involved. That's the only fuckin' thing you've done for us. I had him picked up after you disappeared, grabbed him right off the street. I mean, finding that blood in Cheney's apartment made this a whole new ball game. Hand me that lighter, will you?"

Charlie gingerly gave Zack the hot lighter. Zack used it and gave it back. "Always sure I'm going to drop it between my legs. Helluva note, don't you think? Anyway, Driscoll told us you were dead. Scared? He was petrified. Even more scared of Jukes and Tateo. They'd been paying him to watch the bar, but they didn't trust him. He claims he doesn't know where they're staying. Tateo always telephones him, either at The Lamplighter or his apartment." Zack rolled down the window and threw out the cigarette butt. "Hardly worth the time, was it?"

The Chevrolet had turned east on Hubert, then north on Hudson. Now it turned west on Laight: a one-way street lined with grey and reddish-brown warehouses from five to ten stories high. Most of the buildings had ornate cornices, black metal fire escapes and rounded brick arches over the windows. Several semitrailers were pushed up to loading docks with high overhead doors and metal roofs or awnings. They crossed Collister. The grey paving stones were littered with cardboard and bits of wood.

At Greenwich and Laight a tractor-trailer had been pulled half across the intersection. And at the other end of the block, at Washington, Charlie saw another truck. Both trucks had red cabs and silver trailers with the name *Townsend* printed across their entire length in fat black letters. Between the two trucks the street was empty, except for several parked cars.

The Chevrolet turned left and stopped in front of a pair of green folding doors. The doors opened. They drove into a garage large enough for about ten vehicles and parked beside three other cars. A policeman stood by one of them, neatly arranging half a dozen small two-way radios on its hood.

"Best we could do on short notice," said Zack, opening his door.

Charlie followed him up some steps and into an office with a large picture window from which they could see most of the street. Two plainclothesmen stood by the window, while a third sat on a long work-table talking into a telephone. He had a red puffy face and red hair. When he saw Zack, he put a hand over the mouthpiece and said, "Driscoll gave them the address three minutes ago. I got two men in each truck."

The office was dark with dark oak paneling. On the walls were rows of old photographs showing wagons drawn by teams of six horses. About ten men sat or stood on each wagon, while four more stood by the horses. At the bottom of each picture was written the date and the names of the men in white ink. Against the far wall was a rolltop desk.

Charlie saw a second white Chevrolet pull into the garage. "What do you plan to do?" he asked.

Zack had taken a pink fingernail brush out of his coat pocket and was steadily brushing back his short grey hair. He stood near the two plainclothesmen by the window.

"When Tateo called, Driscoll told him that Sam Cheney had come into the bar and left an envelope with the bartender. Driscoll said he got hold of the envelope and that it contained an address. This address."

"Did he believe him?"

Zack put away the nail brush. "We'll see. The main thing in its favor is that Driscoll isn't supposed to know that Sam Cheney's alive."

The three members of the Yugoslavian fact-finding team entered the room. They carried suitcases, and at first Charlie thought they had chosen this moment to return to their native land. But the suitcases were too thin, no more than four inches deep; and too long, about four feet by one foot. They were covered with brown, leather-like plastic and each had three brass locks. The three men put the cases on the table and unlocked them. Snapping open, the locks made a half-musical pinging noise.

The insides of the cases were lined with grey convoluted foam rubber. It made the rifles with their telescopic sights look like thin men in their coffins.

Charlie joined Zack by the window. "What about the guy with the cocaine?" he asked.

"No trouble there. We spotted him when he opened his mailbox and followed him back to a midtown hotel. When he and Cheney get together, we'll grab 'em."

As he spoke, Zack watched the three members of the SWAT team, special weapons and tactics. "Things used to be a lot simpler," he told Charlie. Then he walked over to the red-haired man on the telephone. "Any word yet?"

"No. We'll pick 'em up when they cross Canal Street or West Broadway. How many grey Valiants are there?"

"Millions. Shit, we don't even know which way they're coming from. Tell those guys to start their trucks."

"Will do."

Despite the pressure, Charlie was aware of a certain calm. He wondered if Texas Ranger John B. Jones had been this businesslike as he waited for Sam Bass's gang in Roundtree, Texas, or what Ranger Frank Hamer had thought about while waiting in ambush for Bonnie and Clyde near Gibland, Louisiana.

Behind him, Charlie could hear the three snipers quietly discussing the merits of a Sako-Finnbear four-shot 7mm magnum with a Redfield 4x–12x variable scope.

"Strongest bolt action rifle around," said the one with the small grey moustache. "Handmade French walnut stock. Just look at that checkering."

"Hollow points?" asked the sniper with the glasses.

"Banana peels."

206

"Fuckin' A."

"Ever try wasp-waisted sonics?" asked the one with the pipe.

"One-eighties?"

"One-fifties are good enough in a .308."

"Give me banana peels every time," said the sniper with the moustache. "See this Monte Carlo cheek piece? Class, that's what I like."

"Come on, you guys," said Zack, "pick up your radios and get upstairs. You, Harris, take your banana peels across the street. Schmidt will let you in. We got about five minutes."

The snipers picked up their rifles and left the room. Charlie was sorry they weren't Yugoslavs.

"Where's Sam and Stacy?" he asked.

Zack had just lit the other half of his Lucky Strike, nearly burning his lips and fingers. He rubbed his mouth with the back of his hand. "If I make it dangerous enough, maybe I'll quit. Cheney's over on East 32nd. His buddy's got an apartment there. The girl's down in the Village. NYU. Been going around talkin' to the eggheads. Think she'll stay?"

"I don't know," said Charlie. But he began to consider what would happen if Sam were arrested and Stacy remained free. The thought took his breath, and he again told himself that she had been friendly only because of Sam.

The red-haired man began talking excitedly into the telephone. "Okay, okay. Great. Hey, Lieutenant, that grey Valiant's on West Broadway."

Zack walked to the door and called to someone in the garage. "Tell Harris to wait 'til they've had a chance to surrender. Those guys upstairs too. They got those trucks running? Okay, tell 'em to get ready."

Coming back into the room, he unbuttoned the top button of his tan shirt and loosened his tie. "The more complicated something gets," he told Charlie, "the more there is to fuck up. It's a fact of life. I'd feel better if they hadn't done such a neat job of shooting that dog."

Charlie, Zack and the man on the telephone were the only ones left in the office. "You still have someone at The Lamplighter?" Charlie asked.

Zack shook his head. "No need."

"Here they come," said the red-haired man.

Charlie and Zack ducked down by the picture window. Charlie was mildly irritated with himself for feeling grateful to Zack, as if the lieutenant's decision to bring him along was based on a new-found sense of comradeship rather than the suspicion that he might contact Sam or Stacy.

It was shortly after noon and the street was brightly sunlit. There were no shadows except along the edge of the opposite warehouses and under the roofs of the loading docks. Harris had crawled to the edge of the roof directly across from them. Charlie could just make him out next to one of the support cables which ran from the loading dock roof up to the fourth story of the warehouse.

Bits of paper and excelsior blew down the street in the spring breeze. Two Styrofoam cups appeared to be chasing each other and six sparrows quarreled over a slice of bread. At the top of the fire escape of a warehouse across the street, someone had set out a number of green plants. There was a false pastoral quality to the scene. Charlie was certain that every other street in the area was crowded with workers eating their lunches, drinking coffee or beer. Whatever Tateo's faults, Charlie didn't think he was stupid. Then he saw the grey Valiant.

It had just passed the red cab of the first semi and drove slowly down the center of the street. Charlie saw the rubber

208

dice swinging from the rearview mirror, but beyond the dice he could only make out two thin shapes, almost silhouettes. He imagined Tateo in his sunglasses and jeans jacket, Jukes with his yellowish-orange hair and red tie-tack earring. The Valiant slowed until Charlie guessed it was going no more than five miles per hour. It had come a dozen yards past the semi. Now it edged forward ten more feet and stopped. There was no movement inside. From where he crouched, Charlie could barely hear the sounds of traffic from the West Side Elevated Highway. The Valiant sat in the middle of the street, sunlight shimmering off its grey hood.

"Too fucking suspicious," said Zack.

There was a roar as the semi at Washington and Laight surged forward. Then there was a second roar as the semi nearest the Valiant began to pull across the intersection at Greenwich. But instead of one smooth motion, it lunged, then stopped, lunged and stopped. Then it stalled.

With a screech of its tires, the Valiant shot backward, aiming for the gap between the semi and the opposite brick wall. Sunlight reflected off its windshield, making it impossible to see inside. Then Charlie saw a hand holding a black gun reach out of the side window and point back toward the red cab of the semi. A steady whirring noise came from the truck as the driver tried to start the stalled engine. This was interrupted by the high crack of a pistol, then again, and a third time.

"You dumb son-of-a-bitch!" shouted Zack.

The lieutenant ran out of the office. As Charlie followed him, he heard explosions from upstairs and across the street which drowned out the noise of the pistol. The rifle shots echoed and reverberated between the warehouses, making an almost continuous roar.

When Charlie next saw the Valiant, he thought its wind-

209

shield was covered with giant dandelion clocks. Then there was another explosion and the windshield disappeared; another explosion and the hood slammed up, hiding the windshield altogether.

The whirring noise was still coming from the truck. There was a sputtering cough, then a whirring noise again. Charlie couldn't see the driver. Presumably he had ducked down to avoid being hit, although the pistol had stopped firing. The rifle shots continued and clang-crashed through the hood of the Valiant or ricocheted off its top with a whine.

Again there was a sputtering cough, then another which developed into a roar. The semi lunged forward. But the Valiant was too close. It swerved briefly as its front tire exploded, then it straightened only a few feet short of the gap and weaved through it. Seconds too late, the truck surged across the opening and slammed into the brick wall of the warehouse bringing a small cascade of bricks and mortar clanging down on its red hood. The explosions stopped. Dropping to one knee, Charlie looked under the trailer and saw the Valiant weaving backward up the next block. He ran after Zack.

The driver of the truck climbed down from his cab. He had blood on his face and more blood dripped from his left arm. He was a young man about Sam's age with blond hair and frightened brown eyes. The truck's windshield was smashed but whether from bullets or falling bricks Charlie didn't know. The young man began apologizing to Zack, apparently thinking that Zack meant to punish him. Zack ignored him and ducked under the trailer.

As Charlie went under the trailer, he heard a honking and screech of brakes, then a crash further up the block. At first he worried about Zack, but coming out from under the truck he saw the policeman still running. Beyond him, however, a green Volkswagen had spun around in a half circle and crashed against a loading dock. Across from it, on the north side of the street, the Valiant was tilted halfway up a set of wide stone steps. Above it the top of a streetlight swung in slow circles.

Zack ran with his gun in his right hand. His brown suit coat flapped behind him and his left arm was outstretched for balance. A horn was blaring; it had a high despairing sound. Charlie saw men staring from windows and standing in the doorways of loading platforms. He began to feel vulnerable and slowed down behind Zack.

"Stay back!" shouted the police lieutenant. "Stay back, they've got guns!"

The warning was unnecessary. Tateo had disappeared. Jukes sat in the front seat, covered with glass from the broken windshield. His hands lay in his lap, fingers curled upward as if waiting for a small offering. His face was completely gone.

Staring at him through the empty windshield, Charlie thought of the hole in the head of a needle. The body was slouched down, and through the head Charlie could see blood-covered springs and the cotton stuffing of the seat. Blood was mixed with the yellowish-orange hair, and the red tie-tack earring seemed like just another drop of it. Charlie backed away. Steam rose from the radiator of the Valiant. The horn was still blowing.

"What a fuck-up," said Zack. "Look at those clowns."

Looking back, Charlie saw the three snipers jogging toward them, holding their rifles across their chests. Their neck ties flapped back over their shoulders. They were laughing and joking among each other.

"You dumb sons-a-bitches, where'd you learn to shoot?"

Charlie touched Zack's arm. "You better do something about Driscoll."

37

BUT WHEN THEY reached The Lamplighter, they found a small crowd gathered outside. Two patrol cars were parked diagonally at the curb, their lights still flashing. A young patrolman was urging people to go home. No one paid any attention. Someone had turned off the large neon sign and the green Molson's ale sign in the window.

Neither Zack nor Charlie said anything as they got out of the white Chevrolet. They walked quickly toward the bar. Charlie could hear sirens in the distance. Above the door was a picture of an old man in a cocked hat lighting a street lamp with a long taper.

As Charlie entered behind Zack, he noticed a broken glass on the floor near the foot of the U-shaped bar. The glass was mixed with a chocolate-colored liquid, and Charlie knew it was a Black Russian.

Four customers, all retired or middle-aged men he had seen before, were gathered in a booth to his right trying to tell another young patrolman what had happened. A third patrolman spoke with Luke, the bartender, while a fourth stood nervously by Driscoll's body at the rear left of the room. The red, blue and yellow rotating lights along with the theater posters of *Damn Yankees* and *Pajama Game* made the policemen seem particularly obtrusive.

"What'd I tell you," said Zack. "A fuck-up."

A siren died away into a whine as another police car pulled up outside. Three plainclothesmen entered the bar.

"Homicide," said Zack.

The officer in charge was a stocky middle-aged man in a dark blue raincoat and dapper Irish tweed hat.

"This your baby?" he asked Zack.

"Not if I can help it."

"What's the story?"

Zack shook his head. "Just got here myself."

The policemen spent about five minutes poking around and talking to the patrolmen, then they took Luke back to the rear right side of the bar. The bartender had already told his story several times and most of his fear had gone out of it. Thin, bald, white shirt and apron, black pants: he looked like he was aspiring to a better place. By now he had realized this was an important moment in his life: his name would be in the papers, business would improve. He didn't appear to recognize Charlie, and spoke directly to Zack and the homicide detective whom Zack called Jonesy.

Luke began by raising his hands and pressing them against his chest. "Who'd want to hurt him? He was one of the nicest men you'd ever want to meet. Been coming in here ten–twelve years. Everybody liked him. Quiet, never any trouble. Now and then he'd have one too many, who doesn't? And I'd say, Mr. Driscoll, time to go home, sir. And he'd give me a smile and say, Thanks, Luke, you're a pal. Then he'd go home. Maybe he'd even leave a tip if he remembered or had anything left."

"What is this," said Jonesy, "memory lane? Save it for the papers."

Luke held out his palms to the policemen. His gold cufflinks were in the shape of tiny locomotives. "What can I say? You asked me what happened, I'm telling you. We

213

got a respectable place here. Never even had a hold-up."
He raised his hands higher as Jonesy began to interrupt.
"Okay, okay. Mr. Driscoll, he was sitting at the end of the
bar, just where he always sits. Been there two–three hours,
drinking more than's usual. Did it relax him, you ask? No
it didn't. He was jumpy as two peas in a pod.

"Then this young guy comes into the bar, wearing sunglasses and dressed up like a cowboy. 42nd Street, right?
Guy never opened his mouth, but Mr. Driscoll heard the
door and turned around. He knew him right off. When he
saw this young guy, he screamed. I kid you not. He
screamed and half fell, half jumped off his stool and ran
toward the back of the bar. This guy that came in, this
cowboy, he takes off his dark glasses very slowly and pulls
a gun from his belt . . ."

"What kind?" asked Jonesy.

"Beats me. A little black jobby. Anyway, he aims it, still
moving slowly, and shoots. I guess he hit Driscoll in the leg
because he fell against the Foos Ball table. Mr. Driscoll
never stopped screaming. Just sounds, know what I mean?
Between you and me, it's gonna be a long time before I
forget it." Luke wiped his hands on his white apron as if
he hoped the memory were like so much spilled beer.

"Then this young guy walked up to him. Still slow, like
he had all the time in the world. Mr. Driscoll kept making
that screaming sound, kept trying to climb back up on the
Foos Ball table. He didn't have a chance. The young guy
shot him three times in the stomach. Then he stuck his gun
in his belt, put on his dark glasses and kept going out the
back door. Never looked at the rest of us, which was all
right by me. Poor Mr. Driscoll though, he was still screaming, but it was quieter, like he was in some other room.
Then it got quieter still, like he was right out of the building. Then it stopped. That was all, it just stopped."

214

After a moment, Charlie walked around the bar toward the Foos Ball table. A patrolman stood near the body, trying not to look at it, but unable to turn completely away. Driscoll lay on his back on the table, his right hand cast backward, his left on his chest. His feet just touched the floor while his head hung over the other side. Strands of grey hair dangled down like wisps of grey ribbon.

Driscoll's body had bent the bars on the table and had broken off several miniature red and blue soccer players that lay in his blood like additional victims. Moving closer, Charlie saw that the blood had divided into two streams that disappeared into the holes by the two miniature goalies. Blood dripped from the bottom of the table to the floor.

Driscoll wore his dark green blazer and light green turtleneck. With his back bent over the table, his large stomach was thrust upward like the curve of a rubber ball. There were three bullet holes in his stomach, each surrounded by a dark powder burn. Blood still oozed from the wounds.

Driscoll's whole face expressed pain. His eyes were open and his eyebrows were raised as if doubting the fact of his death. There was the smell of excrement and urine. Charlie reached forward and closed Driscoll's eyelids.

He was aware of Zack standing behind him. "The guy with the cocaine," said Zack, "he just left his hotel."

38

"MUST OF DUCKED through the warehouse and picked up the Eighth Avenue at Canal Street, then transferred uptown at Fulton. I put a man on it, but it's a dead horse. Probably have better luck at Port Authority." Zack reached out for the padded dash as the white Chevrolet skidded to a halt before a laundry truck which had cut in front of them at 25th Street. Bellevue Hospital was on their right.

The driver revved the siren and the laundry truck moved slowly out of their path. With a screech of its tires, the Chevrolet accelerated up First Avenue.

The man with the cocaine had gone to an apartment house across from Central Park where he was apparently waiting for Sam. Zack had taken over a vacant apartment in the same building. They were going there now from The Lamplighter. Charlie was in the back seat between two plainclothesmen. Zack was in front with the driver. It was 1:45.

"Won't he go after Sam?" asked Charlie.

Zack kept his hands on the dashboard. "How's he know where he is? He thought he was dead until last night."

Charlie was still dissatisfied, but he attributed his doubts

216

to his guilt at having exposed Sam to Tateo. He thought of the eleven o'clock bus, which by now was more than half-way to Saratoga.

The Chevrolet was going as fast as it could without using its siren. The driver kept one hand on the horn, and grinned happily, as if his whole life had been a preparation for this moment. The road dipped slightly at intersections and the Chevrolet swooped into them, making it feel more like a boat than an automobile.

Trying not to look at the road, Charlie asked, "Sam's still on East 32nd?"

"Yeah, but he should be leaving soon. When he makes his buy, we'll have as clean a bust as you'd ever hope to see. You feel bad about his going to jail?"

Charlie felt worse about seeing him trapped and arrested. "Where's Stacy?" he asked.

"Still at NYU."

"If she stays down there, will you leave her alone?"

"Can't tell yet. That apartment where the guy's waiting is rented by someone named Doyle. He and his family have been in Europe for a month, and they're not expected back until the first. Your girlfriend must of had a key. I figure we got enough for a conspiracy charge. Probably pull her in and let the lawyers fight over it."

Charlie again considered what would happen if she didn't join Sam. Perhaps he could speak to the lawyers. If Stacy gave evidence, then the prosecutor might drop charges. But Charlie couldn't imagine her testifying against Sam.

The white Chevrolet was now going north on Madison Avenue, swerving from lane to lane. Charlie kept bumping against the policemen on either side of him. The man on his left didn't seem to mind. He stared out his window and yawned. The plainclothesman on his right, however, winced each time the driver blew the horn.

Seeing Charlie had noticed, he became apologetic. "I've always hated these rides. Must have a weak stomach or something. Some fuckin' delivery truck will squeeze a light and then where are you? Right after lunch, too."

The driver slowed as a yellow taxi cut him off, then he moved up behind the taxi's back bumper and blew his horn. Although Charlie liked Madison Avenue, he found it difficult to play the role of tourist in a speeding car. Just as he was trying to get a better look of the back of St. Patrick's Cathedral, the Chevrolet weaved around a bus, braked for a bicycle, changed lanes and surged forward again, sending Charlie against the shoulder of the plainclothesman on his right.

The man grunted. He had a round, smooth face and a shaggy gunfighter moustache of the sort affected by the three Earp brothers.

"You been around here long?" he asked. "Haven't seen you before."

"I'm just visiting."

Zack turned around in his seat. "Visiting, hell, he's under arrest, practically. Thinks he's Pat Garrett."

"Who?"

"Pat Garrett," said Zack.

"I knew a Garrett in the army," said the plainclothesman after a moment. "Everyone called him Smitty. Never did know why." He began to say something else, then turned and looked out his window instead.

"You going to let the lawyers fight over me too?" asked Charlie. He tried to make a joke of it.

"We'll just see how everything works out," said Zack.

"Did you call Saratoga again?"

Zack grinned. There was no humor in it. "I told you, we'll see how everything works out."

Charlie dropped the subject. The plainclothesman with

the Wyatt Earp moustache stared out his window and tried to pretend he had never spoken.

Several minutes later, the Chevrolet turned west on 67th Street. "Park anywhere," said Zack. "They should have cleared a place."

The driver pulled up next to a fire hydrant. The five men got out, and Zack led the way toward Fifth Avenue. The plainclothesman with the moustache tried to put as much distance as possible between himself and Charlie. As he followed him, Charlie decided that his moustache was much shorter than the ones worn by the Earps, unless perhaps Virgil's. It was more like Tom Horn's moustache. Horn was a one-time lawman and Pinkerton operative who had realized there was better money to be made as a hired killer and switched sides. He was accused of killing several dozen men before being brought to trial in Cheyenne. In jail, he wrote his memoirs (*Life of Tom Horn, Government Scout and Interpreter, Written by Himself: A Vindication*), wove the rope that would hang him and finally shaved off his gunfighter moustache. Charlie considered telling the plainclothesman about Tom Horn but thought better of it.

On the corner was a grey, fourteen-story apartment building with a red awning over its entrance on 67th Street. Zack opened the large glass door. Charlie and the moustached plainclothesman followed him, while the two others continued toward Fifth Avenue. There was no doorman in sight. They passed through a highly polished lobby to a waiting elevator.

Getting off at the third floor, Zack turned left down a short hallway and knocked on a door that was opened by a uniformed patrolman. He stood back to let them pass.

Charlie found himself in a large living room which smelled of paint. The floor and furniture were covered with white dropcloths. The walls were being painted light blue,

219

covering a light yellow which, Charlie thought, looked quite new.

"Beggars can't be choosers," said the man with the Tom Horn moustache.

The only uncovered furniture consisted of three paint-spotted step ladders and two wooden kitchen chairs. The red-haired plainclothesman from the warehouse sat on one of the step ladders talking into a pink princess phone. He nodded to Charlie. Two more plainclothesmen stood by a row of three windows which overlooked Fifth Avenue. To their right was a door to a small balcony. Another row of five windows overlooked 67th Street to Charlie's left. The smell of paint began to give him a headache.

The red-haired man was saying, "He just got here, I told you, hold your fuckin' horses." He handed the phone to Zack. "Max," he said.

Charlie wandered over to the window. Across the street was a larger-than-life bronze statue of seven doughboys charging with fixed bayonets. Actually only three were charging. Two or three others had been shot and the last was supporting one of the wounded. The sun shone on it, emphasizing the dark green of the bronze. In the park behind the statue was a children's playground the size and shape of a hockey rink with red, blue and yellow swings and slides and red, blue and yellow benches for mothers. Charlie was reminded of the colored lights of The Lamplighter. To his left he could see the line of buildings on Central Park South beginning with the Plaza Hotel. Charlie tried to see the zoo, but he wasn't high enough.

"Hey, Bradshaw," said Zack, still holding the telephone, "I've got some bad news for you."

"What is it?" Charlie moved away from the window.

"The girl just joined Sam Cheney on 32nd Street."

Although he had been expecting it, Charlie was startled

220

by the strength of his disappointment. He realized that some part of him had still hoped to run away with Stacy, whether to the Yukon or Far Rockaway, it didn't matter. He felt grief, and it occurred to him that what had died was his own hope of ever experiencing a youthful emotion: whether love or infatuation, that didn't matter either. But even as he thought this, he guessed that his feelings had little to do with the woman who had joined Sam on 32nd Street.

Then another thought occurred to him. "Did she stop by her apartment?"

"What's it matter?"

"Tateo knew she was Sam's girlfriend. He might have been watching her building."

Zack began talking quickly into the phone. Charlie returned to the window and stood looking down at the children's playground. A fat child in a blue parka was swinging back and forth by himself, opening and closing his mouth as if singing some grand song.

"Charlie," said Zack, "the girl left her building at 1:20, carrying a small red suitcase."

Charlie walked back to the center of the room. He thought of Sam on the lightship *Ambrose*, and Sam's statement that Tateo would kill him and that it would be Charlie's fault. "I don't want to tell you your business," said Charlie, "but you'd better check and see if any cars have been stolen near her apartment or The Lamplighter."

"I've already done it."

"Hurry up and wait," said the man with the Tom Horn moustache. "Story of my life."

"Shut the fuck up," said Zack.

39

THE THREE SNIPERS were unhappy. As they entered the apartment carrying their thin rifle cases, they criticized Zack for what they considered his lack of professionalism.

"First he badmouths us and says we're done," said Harris, the sniper with the Sako-Finnbear, "then he grabs us just as we're about to go eat and says he needs us again."

"No fuckin' respect," said the one with the glasses.

The sniper with the pipe put his case down on the white dropcloth covering the floor, and removed his rifle: a Mossberg .308. "Never trust a man who don't know his own mind," he said.

"Does he want us on the roof?" asked Harris. He, too, had taken out his rifle and began to load it.

"Too high," said the one with the glasses. "We're to shoot from the windows."

The sniper with the pipe rubbed his Mossberg with a clean white cloth. "Get a nice shot from the balcony there."

"Too public," said Harris. "Somebody might bitch."

The snipers didn't acknowledge Charlie or the plainclothesman on the phone or the plainclothesman Charlie had embarrassed in the car. Zack had gone down to the street to tell his men not to look like "sore thumbs."

222

Charlie realized that no matter who else was nearby, the snipers always gave the sense of being alone. Even when Zack spoke to them, they barely paid attention. He imagined them as not speaking to anyone who scored less than 495 out of 500 bull's-eyes. Once Charlie had seen a man with a Marlin .22 hit the edge of a playing card, cutting it in half, ten times out of ten from a distance of thirty feet. He wondered if such skill with instruments of death kept the snipers from seeing lesser men as among the living.

Zack reentered the room. He had lost the businesslike calm that he had had at the warehouse, and his movements had become quick and abrupt. "That fuckhead upstairs, he's just sitting there watching the TV. Maybe he plans to move in. Harris, get by that side window. You two stick to the front. You're looking for the guy you missed earlier. Remember that? Nobody else. Keep those fucking guns out of the window or you'll be doing your shooting at Coney Island from now on. Hey, Bradshaw, your buddy Sam Cheney have a gun?"

"No," said Charlie.

"I thought he swiped yours."

"I got it back." Charlie didn't care to say that it was at the bottom of the East River.

The phone rang and the red-haired man answered it. After a moment he told Zack, "They just left 32nd Street in a blue, 1967 four-door Plymouth."

"Is Stacy with them?" Charlie tried to keep his voice calm.

"The girl? I'll check." He relayed the question, then paused and said, "Yeah, the girl's with them."

"Let me talk to him." Zack took the phone. "Carter? Is there any chance they're being followed by another car?" Zack looked at Charlie and shrugged. "What do you mean, you can't be positive?" Charlie joined Zack by the phone.

"What d'you mean 'reasonably positive'?" Zack said. "What the hell am I to do with that? Okay, okay, just make sure, that's all." He gave the phone back to the red-haired man. "Dumb fuck."

"Arrest them now," said Charlie, "don't wait for them to get here."

"I want to get him making his buy."

"You're risking his life."

"He's doing that all by himself," said Zack.

Charlie started to reach out and take Zack's arm, then he stopped himself. "Did you learn anything about stolen cars?"

Zack moved away from him. "There are two from that general area, but that doesn't mean anything. Even if he stole a car, we probably wouldn't get a report on it until after five. Personally, I don't think this Tateo guy is after them."

"Keep hoping," said Charlie.

The three snipers had opened their windows and pulled down the shades, leaving about six inches of space. Through the windows Charlie could hear the traffic on Fifth Avenue: cars and buses stopping for the light, then pulling away. Occasionally he could hear the shouts of children from the playground. He walked over to the window between the two snipers.

Looking down, he could see about twenty kids, none more than six or seven, on the swings and teeter-totters, scrambling over the red and blue jungle jim, playing in the sandbox. It was about 2:45 and the temperature had reached the mid-fifties. Charlie thought he could even see buds on the trees. The child in the blue parka now stood on the pedestal of the statue of the charging doughboys, maintaining his balance by holding on to a bronze bayonet.

The snipers had knelt down by their windows. Across the

224

room by the side windows, Harris was quietly whistling *Get Me to the Church on Time.*

"Fuckin' trees," said the sniper with the pipe. "Hey, Zack, couldn't you pick a better place. Your guy runs into the park and those trees will give us real grief."

Zack ignored him.

"Get the mayor to cut them down," said the sniper with glasses.

"Lieutenant," said the man on the phone, "that blue Plymouth just crossed 62nd on Madison."

Charlie began to pay particular attention to four or five men spread out over 100 yards near the low stone wall separating the sidewalk and the park. Although he was certain they were policemen and thought he recognized the driver of the white Chevrolet, he didn't believe they would do any good. He kept seeing Driscoll's body draped across the Foos Ball table with three bullet holes in his stomach. Then he imagined Sam dead, or Stacy.

As he crouched by the window, Charlie marvelled at the bungle of events that had begun with his coming to New York to rescue Sam and might conceivably end with getting him killed. However much he might dislike Sam, it was hard not to feel fatherly.

But although he was concerned for Sam, he was frightened for Stacy. Charlie had begun to see her as an innocent victim, and kept telling himself there must have been more he could have done to save her. Although he knew this was foolish, he couldn't stop thinking of her and kept seeing her thin face and the curve of her body in his mind. He regretted a world where there was no place for romantic action, and at times felt lost in that empty area between the films of his childhood and the business of the Saratoga Springs police department.

"Hey, Lieutenant," said the man on the phone, "the blue

225

Plymouth went up and turned on 69th Street. Should be seeing it any minute now."

Going to the window, Zack raised and lowered the shade several times. "What about another car?" he asked.

"Still no sign," said the man on the phone.

Zack joined Charlie between the two snipers. "We only got one car following them. Two or three, we might know something, but there's not much we can do with one." He had taken the pink plastic nailbrush from his coat pocket and was brushing back his grey hair. It seemed a reflex gesture, as if no part of his conscious mind were focused on it.

Charlie stared up Fifth Avenue looking for the blue Plymouth. There was a lot of traffic, while on the sidewalk about twenty people were walking dogs, pushing baby carriages or just strolling along in the spring weather.

"Too bad we can't arrange these things for rainy days," said Zack.

"You just better hope your snipers are accurate." Charlie was still angry at Zack for refusing to arrest Sam earlier.

"Nah, I'll bet you ten bucks we get him at Port Authority."

Charlie didn't answer. He had just seen the blue Plymouth. It was behind a bus on the far side of Fifth, closer to 68th than 67th. Dented and repainted, it looked like one of those cars that had grown old as a yellow cab before being sold with 200,000 miles on its rebuilt engine. The driver was carefully obeying all the laws. He drew up to the curb by the light and stopped. After a moment, Sam and Stacy got out. The Plymouth pulled away. Charlie told himself that if they could only get across Fifth and into the building, they would be safe.

Sam and Stacy stood waiting for the light to change. Sam held a brown attaché case. The wind blowing across the park blew his black hair into his eyes. He wore a brown corduroy jacket and corduroy jeans. Charlie could just make out his turquoise and silver necklace. He guessed that the brown corduroy had some political significance, that somebody in a bar had once told Sam about people wearing brown corduroy in Portugal or Cambodia or Hanoi.

"Okay," said Zack to the man on the phone, "tell 'em to get the guy in the Plymouth. He should be circling the block." The red-haired man relayed his instructions. "Jesus, what are they waiting for?"

The wind flicked Stacy's hair around her face in a small black cloud. She had on jeans and a yellow sweater. Charlie tried to read some emotion into the way she was standing —fear or excitement—but she simply looked like someone waiting to cross the street. Neither she nor Sam made any attempt to cross against the light even though the traffic had cleared.

Glancing up Fifth, Charlie noticed a green Econoline van weaving across the three lanes of traffic toward the park, cutting off a taxi that began honking indignantly. The van was rusty and dust-covered. At one time someone had taken off its front bumper and replaced it with several black two-by-six boards. Through the van's front window, Charlie could see a young man in a jeans jacket. The cab driver kept honking his horn.

"That's him!" said Charlie.

"Son-of-a-bitch!"

"Lieutenant," said the man on the phone, "they think maybe a green . . ."

Charlie ran to the door of the balcony, pulled it open and stepped to the edge where there was a black metal fence. "Run!" he shouted. "Run!"

But Sam and Stacy were already running toward the

park. Reaching the intersection, the van crashed up over the curb, barely passing between a tree and a lightpole. There was a rasping noise as its tailpipe scraped along the concrete. It braked, screeching to a halt. Its rear end slewed around to the left and smashed into a litter barrel, knocking it into Fifth Avenue and sending paper and trash up into the wind.

Tateo was out of the truck before it had come to a complete stop. He ran toward the park, holding a small black gun in his right hand.

Charlie could hear Zack shouting. "Bust the guy upstairs! Don't hurt him. No, nobody's buying a fuckin' thing!"

The sniper with the pipe suddenly appeared on the balcony. He fell to his stomach and shoved his rifle through the bars of the railing.

"Too many trees and civilians. Can't get a fuckin' aim."

Sam and Stacy were already past the entrance to the playground. Charlie could see Stacy's yellow sweater moving jerkily through the trees like a banner or warning. Tateo had vaulted the low stone wall and was weaving and twisting between the bushes and shrubbery toward the park sidewalk. His jean jacket flapped open behind him and he held his pistol up over his head, more like a torch than a weapon. As Tateo jumped and side-stepped around the bushes, Charlie was reminded of a lean hunting animal. Now other men were running toward the van or the park entrance.

"Still can't get a bead," said the sniper.

Charlie stood gripping the railing. There was an explosion from inside the apartment and a small evergreen blew apart to the right of Tateo.

"Make fucking sure!" shouted Zack.

Sam and Stacy had cut across the grass up a small rise

228

topped with several large rocks. Beyond them to their left was a slight decline and a sidewalk leading to a tunnel under one of the roads crossing the park. The tunnel emerged by the children's zoo. Ten more feet and they would be on the other side of the rise. Sam was a few feet ahead of Stacy. He still held the brown attaché case.

Tateo had dropped to one knee on the far side of a line of green benches just past the entrance to the playground. He raised the pistol, holding it with both hands. Sam and Stacy were at the top of the rise.

"Now the fuckin' bench's in the way," said the sniper.

There was another explosion from inside the apartment and a large chunk of wood flew up from the bench behind Tateo.

Charlie saw the pistol jerk in Tateo's hand, then he heard a slight crack, small and insubstantial, almost hidden by the sounds of traffic and shouting that came from the park. He couldn't believe it would cause any harm, something that small.

Stacy had stopped and stood swaying at the top of the rise. Her arms were outstretched toward Sam who had disappeared over the other side. She took a small step, then another, like a child learning to walk. Then, without bending her knees, she slowly fell forward onto the grass.

Sam reappeared at the top of the rise and ran back toward Stacy. He seemed small, the size of someone on a television screen. He held his left hand out in front of him as if to protect himself or warn someone away or simply give up. His mouth was open but Charlie couldn't hear any sound.

Zack appeared at the door of the balcony. "What the fuck you doing?" he shouted.

"I think I got a bead on him now," said the sniper.

There was another thin cracking noise. Charlie saw Sam

twist, swinging the attaché case in a wide arc, and stumble backwards toward the rocks. The pistol shot was immediately followed by an explosion at Charlie's feet. Tateo was flung up and sent sprawling as if he had been kicked.

"Nice," said the sniper.

40

BY THE TIME Charlie reached the park, uniformed policemen had appeared and were already pushing away the crowd. The green Econoline van half blocked the sidewalk, its engine still running. Two little girls with blond hair and matching red jackets stood on tiptoe to see in its front window.

Charlie ran through the entrance of the park and past a green sign reading, "This is your park *please* help us keep it clean." Low shrubbery bordered the sidewalk. A plainclothesman hurried by in the opposite direction. To his right Charlie noticed about ten children watching from behind the black iron bars of the playground, while beyond them several mothers were herding more children back toward the swings.

Charlie stopped by a blue wooden box containing trashcans. There was a sign on a lamp post warning people to keep their dogs on leashes. Near the benches ahead of him a group of five men surrounded something on the ground.

Moving forward, Charlie approached the men. Then one of them stepped aside and Charlie saw Tateo lying with his arms and legs apart: a blue X-shape on the leaves and brown grass. A black automatic lay a few inches beyond the reach of his right hand.

There was no question that he was dead. The top of his head was completely gone, making it seem as if he had dyed his brown hair red to match the hair of his dead friend. He had been thrown forward with such force that one of his cowboy boots had been pulled half off and lay twisted upward, as if his ankle had been broken as well.

Charlie hurried past Tateo's body and up the rise toward Stacy. She lay on her back with two policemen bending over her. She kept turning her head back and forth, back and forth, and as she turned her black hair was tossed up and around her face, half hiding it. Her eyes were open and she seemed to stare at the trees or sky. Her mouth was open but she made no noise. There was a red, widening stain on her yellow sweater.

Charlie looked for Sam and saw him about fifteen feet away further along the rise. He was alone, although a policeman was walking toward him. Sam was on all fours and crawling very slowly. His head hung down and his black hair brushed the ground. He wasn't crawling toward Stacy or the attaché case, but in some new third direction as if he had chosen this moment in which to change his life.

Two, three, four more people were walking toward him. They didn't stop him, but watched him crawl across the brown grass toward the tunnel under the road. Then a uniformed policeman reached out and gently touched Sam's shoulder. Sam collapsed, toppling forward onto his right side. His legs kept moving, however, pumping slowly up and down, like a turtle that's been turned over on its back and is still trying to walk. His face was pinched and cringing. He, too, had a widening red stain on his white Indian shirt.

Looking at him, Charlie thought of a photograph he had once seen of Bob and Grat Dalton after they had been caught robbing the bank in Coffeyville, Kansas, and had been shot down with their gang in Death Alley. The photograph showed six men trying to hold up the bodies of the two outlaws: knees collapsing, hands against their stomachs, eyes crinkled shut.

Bob Dalton's last words had been to his brother Emmett, who was trying to save him: "Don't mind me, boy. I'm done for. Don't surrender! Die game!"

The plainclothesman with the Tom Horn moustache took off his sport coat, folded it and put it under Sam's head.

Charlie went back to where Stacy lay surrounded now by about half a dozen people. She was still turning her head back and forth. Charlie sat down on the ground beside her and began stroking her forehead, pushing her hair out of her face. Although her eyes were open, she didn't appear to see him. Slowly, however, she stopped moving her head. Charlie stayed beside her, looking down at her and stroking her head. The sky was warm and blue. A small black child ran in circles shouting, "Bang, bang, bang!" There were sirens on Fifth Avenue.

Zack joined the small crowd of people around Charlie and Stacy. "What'd I tell you?" he said. "A fuck-up."

SATURDAY

41

THE BUS THAT TOOK Charlie back to Saratoga
Springs was a Greyhound and continued on to Montreal.
For nearly four hours he had been half aware of passengers
speaking quietly in French. It seemed a civilized and peace-
ful language. As the bus pulled into the Spa City Diner,
Charlie began to think of going on to Montreal.

He had talked to Marge on the phone the previous
evening. She had been worried and urged him to come
home. She had not heard again from Chief Peterson and
knew nothing about Charlie's future with the police department. Whatever happened, she told him, they could count
on his cousins for help. That had not pleased him, but he
had been moved by her concern.

Nor had he been pleased by Zack who had said he would
call Chief Peterson as long as Charlie promised not to talk
to reporters. It would never have occurred to Charlie to
talk to reporters, but he was angry at Zack's bungling of
events and even angrier at Zack's insistence that he be a
witness to it. Charlie had told the police lieutenant not to
do him any favors. He didn't care to be beholden to a man
he disliked.

Tateo, Jukes and Driscoll were dead. Sam and Stacy were
in the hospital. They would recover but go to jail. The

driver of the Plymouth had been arrested, as had the man with the cocaine. When the police had burst into the apart ment, he had said only, "I didn't think this would work."

And now Charlie was thinking about Montreal. He imagined sitting back and continuing north. He could find a job; it wouldn't matter what. Maybe he could learn French. In any case, he wouldn't return to Saratoga.

People began to get off the bus. Looking out into the parking lot, Charlie expected to see police cars with flashing lights or at least his three cousins. The only person he recognized was a frail white-haired old man known generally as Old Mac Davis who spent his life meeting buses, still waiting for someone who should have arrived during the war.

A young couple behind him continued to speak French. Although Charlie had no knowledge of the language, it sounded welcoming. He knew if he went to Montreal, no one would be terribly upset. People would miss him but they would get over it. Even his wife would get over it.

As for himself, he would miss kids' baseball and being a youth officer. He would miss poking around and finding out about things. Maybe he could be a policeman in Montreal. But as he thought this, the stronger memory passed through his mind of Stacy in her yellow sweater lying wounded on the ground. He couldn't stand the idea of her being hurt. He didn't know how he would endure not seeing her again.

The bus driver walked back along the aisle. He nodded to Charlie. "Saratoga Springs," he said. "You getting off?"

The young couple behind him stopped talking. Charlie glanced out the window at Old Mac Davis waiting for someone who would never arrive. The sun was shining. Charlie shrugged and got to his feet, reached up and pulled his green plaid canvas bag from the overhead rack. Then he walked toward the front of the bus.

238

Descending the steps to the parking lot, Charlie was pleased to discover that it was a warm spring day. He paused to look around at the parked cars, the motels and rooming houses across the street. Then he turned toward the diner. He had, after all, found Sam Cheney.

STEPHEN DOBYNS

Stephen Dobyns was born in Orange, New Jersey, in 1941, and raised in New Jersey, Michigan, Virginia and Pennsylvania. He was educated at Shimer College, Wayne State University and the University of Iowa. His jobs have included teaching at various colleges and working as a reporter for the Detroit News. *His book of poems,* Concurring Beasts, *was the Lamont Poetry Selection for 1971. A novel,* A Man of Little Evils, *was published in 1973. He currently lives in New Hampshire.*